Kelly Couldn't Help But Notice His Swagger, Which More Than Did Justice To The Best-Looking Behind She'd Ever Seen.

"Are you sure you really want my help?" she asked.

"You can't jump ship on me now," he said.

"I intend to keep my word." She paused. "I just hope you won't be sorry."

"Oh, I won't be," he said huskily, looking at her as if he could eat her up.

No, she told herself, don't let him mess with you like this. Her feelings were purely physical. If she ignored them, they would go away.

"You know what I'd like to do about now, don't you?" The husky pitch had grown deeper.

That tightening in her chest increased.

"I'd like to kiss the hell out of you."

Dear Reader,

Thanks for taking time out of your hectic life to pick up and enjoy a Silhouette Desire novel. We have six outstanding reads for you this month, beginning with the latest in our continuity series, THE ELLIOTTS. Anna DePalo's *Cause for Scandal* will thrill you with a story of a quiet twin who takes on her identical sister's persona and falls for a dynamic hero. Look for her sister to turn the tables next month.

The fabulous Kathie DeNosky wraps up her ILLEGITIMATE HEIRS trilogy with the not-to-be-missed *Betrothed for the Baby*—a compelling engagement-of-convenience story. We welcome back Mary Lynn Baxter to Silhouette Desire with *Totally Texan*, a sensual story with a Lone Star hero to drool over. WHAT HAPPENS IN VEGAS...is perhaps better left there unless you're the heroine of Katherine Garbera's *Her High-Stakes Affair*—she's about to make the biggest romantic wager of all.

Also this month are two stories of complex relationships. Cathleen Galitz's *A Splendid Obsession* delves into the romance between an ex-model with a tormented past and the hero who finds her all the inspiration he needs. And Nalini Singh's *Secrets in the Marriage Bed* finds a couple on the brink of separation with a reason to fight for their marriage thanks to a surprise pregnancy.

Here's hoping this month's selection of Silhouette Desire novels bring you all the enjoyment you crave.

Happy reading!

Melissa Jeglinski

Melissa Jeglinski
Senior Editor
Silhouette Desire

Please address questions and book requests to:
Silhouette Reader Service
U.S.: 3010 Walden Ave., P.O. Box 1325, Buffalo, NY 14269
Canadian: P.O. Box 609, Fort Erie, Ont. L2A 5X3

MARY LYNN BAXTER

Totally Texan

Published by Silhouette Books

America's Publisher of Contemporary Romance

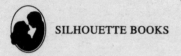 **SILHOUETTE BOOKS**

ISBN 0-373-76713-7

TOTALLY TEXAN

Copyright © 2006 by Mary Lynn Baxter

Printed in U.S.A.

MARY LYNN BAXTER

A native Texan, Mary Lynn Baxter knew instinctively that books would occupy an important part of her life. Always an avid reader, she became a school librarian, then a bookstore owner, before writing her first novel.

Now Mary Lynn Baxter is an award-winning author who has written more than thirty novels, many of which have appeared on the *USA TODAY* list.

Dedicated to Walter G. Bates, forester and friend, who once again gifted me with his immense talent.

One

Grant Wilcox had just stepped out of his truck when Harvey Tipton, the postmaster, walked out of the Sip 'n Snack coffee shop.

Harvey greeted Grant with a grin through his scruffy beard and mustache. "Hey, about to take a look-see, huh? Or maybe I should say another one."

Grant gave him a perplexed look. "What are you talking about?"

"The new piece in town."

Grant made a face. "I'm assuming you're referring to the new woman in town, right?"

"Right," Harvey responded, with his head bobbing up and down, his grin still in place. He obviously saw no reason to be ashamed or to make an apology for his unflattering terminology. "She's running the shop for Ruth."

Of all people to run into, Grant groaned inwardly; Harvey was the town's most prolific gossip. And the fact that he was a man made it worse.

Grant shrugged. "That's news to me, but then I haven't been in for coffee in a while."

"When you see her you'll regret that."

"I doubt it," Grant said wryly.

"I didn't figure you for dead yet, Wilcox."

"Give me a break, will you?" Grant was irritated and didn't bother to hide the fact.

"Well, she's a stunner," Harvey declared. "Heads above anyone else around here."

"So why are you telling me?" Grant asked in a bored tone, hoping Harvey would take the hint.

Harvey gave him a conspiratorial grin. "Thought maybe you might be interested, since you're the only one around here without a wife or significant other." He slapped Grant on the shoulder and widened his grin. "If you know what I mean."

For a second Grant wanted to flatten the postmaster's nose, but of course he didn't. Harvey wasn't the only one who had tried to play matchmaker for him.

Sure, he'd like a hot-blooded, feisty woman to occupy his bed on occasion, but the thought of anything permanent made him break into a chill. For the first time ever, life was good—especially in the small town of Lane, Texas. As a forester, Grant was doing what he loved and that was playing in the woods, cutting trees that would eventually earn him a ton of money.

More than that, he wasn't ready to settle down. With his roaming past, he never knew when the itch to move might strike; then where would he be? Trapped. Nope, that wasn't for him, at least not now.

"So want me to go back in and introduce you?" Harvey asked into the silence, following with a deep belly laugh.

Grant gritted his teeth and said, "Thanks, Harv, but I can take care of myself when it comes to women." He pointedly looked at his watch. "I'm sure you have customers waiting for you."

Harvey winked. "Gotcha."

Yet once the postmaster was out of sight, Grant found himself walking a bit faster toward the entrance to the Sip 'n Snack.

Kelly Baker scrubbed her hands hard in the hot, sudsy water, pulling her lower lip between her teeth. She had been putting pastries in the front counter and was convinced she had goo up to her elbows.

Since she'd been in this small country town of Lane— three weeks now—she'd asked herself over and over if she'd truly lost her mind. She knew the answer, though, and it was no. Her cousin, Ruth Perry, had needed help, and Kelly had come to the rescue, just as Ruth had come to hers following the tragic event that had changed her life forever.

"Ouch," Kelly mumbled, feeling a stinging sensation in her hands. Jerking them out of the water, she grabbed a towel, then frowned as she looked at her fingers. Gone were the long, beautifully manicured nails and the soft skin she was once so proud of. Now, her hands looked all dried and pruney, as if she kept them constantly immersed. She did, even though she had two daytime helpers, Albert and Doris.

Another sigh followed as Kelly looked around the empty

coffee shop, picturing how it would look in a short time. It would be teeming with people. She smiled to herself at the word *teeming*. That term hardly fit this tiny town.

Still, who was she to make fun? Ruth's newest addition to this logging community of two thousand had been a huge hit. With little invested, her cousin was already turning a profit—albeit a small one—selling gourmet coffees, pastries, soups and sandwiches.

According to the locals, Sip 'n Snack was the place to be. And that was good. If Kelly had to be in this place, at least she was where the action was, until the shop closed every day.

Kelly dreaded the evenings. They were far too long and gave her too much time to think. Even though she walked in the door of Ruth's small, cozy house so exhausted she could barely make it to the bathtub, much less to bed, she still couldn't sleep.

But nights had been her problem long before she came to Lane. And now with the empty afternoons, the past had ample opportunity to rear its traumatic head and haunt her once again. Soon, though, she would fulfill her obligation to her cousin an would be back at home in Houston where she belonged.

However, she reminded herself ruefully, her personal life hadn't been any better there or she wouldn't be *here* now. Inside, at the core of her being, her heart had been coated with cement that nothing could chip away.

"Phone for you, Kelly."

When she picked it up, Ruth's cheerful voice said, "Hi, toots, how's it going?"

"It's going."

"I don't want to keep bugging you, but I can't stand not

knowing what's going on. I'm having major withdrawals from the shop."

"I can imagine."

"Have you met him yet?"

Kelly made a face. "Met who?"

Ruth chuckled. "The town hunk, the only single guy worth his salt around there."

Kelly purposely hid her agitation. "If I met him, I didn't know it."

"Oh, trust me, you'd know."

"You're wasting your time, Ruth, playing matchmaker."

Her cousin sighed. "It's past time you looked at other men. *Way* past."

"Who says I don't look?"

"Pooh. You know what I mean."

Kelly laughed. "Hey, don't stress yourself about me. If I'm supposed to find someone else, I will." Only not in this lifetime.

"Sure." Ruth's tone was a tad cynical. "You're just telling me what I want to hear."

Kelly laughed again. "Gotta run. I just heard the buzzer."

Before Ruth could reply, Kelly hung up. Setting her smile in place, she came from behind the counter, only to pull up short and stare. Later, she didn't know why she had behaved in such a manner. Perhaps it was because he was so tall and handsome.

Or better yet, perhaps it was the way he was looking at her.

Was this the "hunk" Ruth had just told her about?

To her chagrin, the stranger's dark blue eyes began at the tip of her toes and worked slowly upward, missing nothing of her trim frame. He gave a pointed glance at her breasts and hair, making her strangely glad she had recently placed highlights in her short, sherry-colored tresses.

When those incredible dark eyes whipped back up to hers, the air was charged with electricity. Stunned, Kelly realized she was holding her breath.

"Like what you see?" she asked before she thought. God, where had that come from? *Her real job*. Being bold and forward was what had pushed her to succeed in her profession.

The big guy grinned, a slow, sexy grin. "As a matter of fact, I do."

For the first time since her husband's death four years prior, Kelly was completely unnerved by a man's stare. And voice. She sensed, however, this stranger wasn't just any man. There was something special about him that commanded attention. *Rugged* was the word that came to mind.

She wasn't used to seeing men in worn jeans, washed so much that their color had faded, plus a flannel shirt, scarred steel-toed boots and a hard hat in his hand. Even in Lane, this caliber of man was rare.

He was still staring at her. Kelly shifted her feet and tried to look away, but failed. That ruggedness seemed to go hand in hand with his six-foot-plus height, muscled body and slightly mussed, sun-kissed brown hair.

Big and dangerous. A treacherous combination.

God, what was she thinking? No matter how attractive or charming the man, she wasn't interested. If so, she would've encouraged other men's affections—in Houston. He was probably up to his armpits in women, anyway, even in Lane.

No man would ever measure up to her deceased

husband, Eddie. Having drawn that conclusion, Kelly had concentrated on her career and made it her reason for living.

Breaking into the growing silence, she asked in her most businesslike tone, "What can I get you?"

"What's the special today?" he asked in a deep, brusque voice that matched his looks.

Kelly cleared her throat, glad some normalcy had returned. "Coffee?"

"That'll do for starters," he responded, striding deeper into the shop, pulling out a chair and sitting down.

"The specials are on the board." To her dismay, Kelly was rooted to the spot like a tongue-tied imbecile. Then, red-faced, she finally whipped her gaze to the board behind the counter, which always listed the day's coffee and food specials.

"Not this time," he drawled, "unless I've lost a day." He paused. "Today's Wednesday, not Tuesday. Right?"

Convinced her face matched the color of her hair, Kelly nodded. She hadn't changed the sign, which under ordinary circumstances wouldn't have been a big deal. But for some reason, this man's comment made her feel inadequate, a condition she despised.

Shrugging her shoulders, Kelly gave him a sugary smile and said, "French vanilla latte is the coffee flavor for the day."

He rubbed his chin for a moment, then frowned. "Too bad a fellow can't just get a plain cup of joe?"

Realizing that he was teasing her, she kept that smile in place and said, "Sorry, this is not that kind of shop. But then you know that. So if it's supermarket coffee you want, you'll have to make your own."

He chuckled. "I know."

Despite her reluctance, she felt a grin toying with her lips.

"I'll take the plain brew that's closest to normal old coffee."

When she returned with the cup and placed it in front of him, Kelly didn't look at him, hoping to discourage further conversation. Despite his good looks, for some reason, this man made her uncomfortable, and she wanted no part of him. Still, she handed him a menu.

He glanced at it, laid it aside, then looked back up at her. "So you're the new Ruth?"

"Hardly."

"So where is she?"

"Out of state caring for her ailing mother."

"You're filling in, huh?"

"For a while, anyway."

His thick eyebrows bunched together as his gaze locked on her again. "By the way, I'm Grant Wilcox."

"Kelly Baker."

Instead of offering his hand, he nodded. "A pleasure."

Every time he spoke, she had a physical reaction to his voice. It was like being struck by something you thought would be severe and bruising, so that you recoiled inwardly. Only it wasn't at all. It was pleasant, in fact.

"You from around here?" he asked after taking a long sip of his coffee.

"No," Kelly said hesitantly. "Actually, I'm from Houston. How about yourself?"

"Not originally. But I am now. I live about ten miles west of town. I own a logging company and recently bought the timber on a huge tract of land. So I'm stuck in Lane. At least for the time being."

The skin around his eyes crinkled when he smiled, and

he was smiling now. "We've just started cutting, and I'm happy as a pig in the sunshine."

Was he deliberately trying to sound like a hick or was he trying to tell her something by using that off-putting terminology? "That's good," she said for lack of anything else to say. Despite her reaction to Grant, intellectually she couldn't care less what he was or what he did. So she asked if he'd like something to eat now.

As if he picked up on her attitude, a smirk crossed his lips, then he said, "I'll have a bowl of soup and a warm-up on my coffee."

All he needed to add was "little lady" to go with that directive. He definitely didn't seem to be the world's most progressive guy. Was it so obvious she was out of her comfort zone? Or was he just intuitive? It didn't matter. What *did* matter was that his condescending manner not only infuriated her, but also made her more determined than ever to serve him with perfection.

Grabbing the pot from behind the counter, Kelly made her way back toward his table, a smile plastered on her lips. She picked up his cup, and that was when it happened. The cup slipped from her hand and its contents landed in Grant Wilcox's lap. He let out a shout.

Speechless with horror, Kelly watched as he kicked back his chair and stood.

"I'd say that was a good shot, lady," he said.

Though her empty hand flew to her mouth, Kelly's eyes dipped south, where they became glued to the wet spot surrounding his zipper.

Then they both looked up at the same time, their gazes locking.

"Fortunately, none the worse for wear," he drawled, a slow smile crawling across his lips.

Horrified, mortified—you name it—Kelly could only stammer, "Oh my God—I'm so sorry." Her voice sounded nothing like her own. "Stay put and I'll get a towel."

Whirling, she practically ran to the counter, When she returned, Grant's eyes met hers again.

"Here, let me," she said, reaching out, only to stop abruptly when she saw the open grin on his face. She yanked her hand back, feeling blood rush into her cheeks.

"That's okay. I think I'll just change my jeans."

"Uh, right," Kelly said after finding her voice.

"How much do I owe you?"

Kelly was appalled that he'd even ask that. "Under the circumstances, absolutely nothing."

He turned then and walked toward the exit. Kelly could only stand spellbound in shock.

When he reached the door he turned and winked. "See ya."

She hoped not. But at the same time, she was sorry, because he *did* have the cutest ass and swagger she'd ever seen—even when he'd just braved hot coffee from her hands.

Too bad they were wasted on her.

Two

He hated paperwork, but that didn't mean he could ignore it.

Grant's gaze cut over to the desk in the corner of the room, and he groaned. Not only were there stacks of invoices that had to be paid, there were folders that needed to be filed.

He'd gone outdoors for a while. Swinging an ax had given him some much-needed physical relief. After spending most of the morning behind closed doors with his banker, reviewing his finances, he'd needed the outlet. Bank sessions nearly always made a nutcase out of him.

A lot of things this morning had made him half-crazy. Following his shower a short time ago, he'd checked his crown jewels for the first time, since their coffee bath that morning, and deduced they were intact and good to go.

Grant snorted. Only problem with the latter, they *had*

no place to go. Better yet, no one to go to. He could barely recall the last time he'd shared a bed with a woman and really enjoyed it. Through the years, few women had had the power to either disturb his libido or hold his interest.

However, he had to admit with brutal honesty that Ruth Perry's replacement, whoever she was, had definitely done both.

Kelly Baker was one fine woman. He couldn't help but notice her fragile porcelain skin with its delicate dusting of freckles. She had wonderful bones, with curves that were just right, and her clothes draped her slender frame to perfection.

Too bad she didn't seem to have a brain to match all those physical assets. A twinge of conscience bit him, telling him that probably wasn't a fair assessment of the woman. They'd spoken for barely two minutes, and he didn't know anything about her but her name. No doubt, though, she was out of her element and didn't have a clue what she was doing in the food business. Under other conditions and circumstances, he might have enjoyed spending time with her.

"Ah, hell, Wilcox," he muttered, reaching for his beer and taking another swig, "give it a rest."

She wouldn't be caught dead with the likes of him. It hadn't taken him but a few seconds to get her number—a city broad with a city attitude. As far as he was concerned, both those things sucked. No way would the two of them ever get together.

Again, that was too bad; she was a looker. He liked women with spunk, and she appeared to have more than her share of that. He'd relish the opportunity to play with a woman like her. For a few days anyway, he mused ruefully. It was okay to dream, just as long as he didn't do something foolish and try to turn those dreams into reality.

He almost laughed aloud at that crazy thought.

No way was he going to mess with that woman. Already there was something about her that was a real turn-on to him. Perhaps it was because she appeared so untouchable, so condescending, that he wanted to explore what lay under that sheet of ice, then prove he was man enough to melt it. First by grabbing her and pressing her against the wall of his chest… He could almost taste her flesh as he imagined himself caressing, nibbling, kissing her mouth, her neck, her shoulders and her back.

What would she feel? Would he make her tingle, make her hot?

Now that was a hoot, thinking she'd ever let him within touching distance. Disgusted with his thoughts of the ice queen, Grant got up, trudged to the kitchen and helped himself to another beer.

It was after he'd killed the contents that the idea struck him. He stood still, feeling heat boil up in him. "Ah, hell, Wilcox. Forget it. That's crazy. You're crazy!"

Crazy or not, he was going to do it. Grabbing a jacket, he headed out the door, knowing that he'd probably lost what mind he had left.

Her face still flamed.

And not from the tub of hot water she'd been soaking in for at least thirty minutes. How could she have done such a thing? How could she have been so clumsy? She never had been at such a loss before. Cool, calm and collected was how she was thought of at the firm, how she generally operated on a day to day basis.

Or at least how she used to, before…

Kelly shook her head, refusing to go there. She had already beaten up on herself enough. To dwell on the now was not only detrimental to her psyche, but stupid. What happened four years ago couldn't be changed. Nothing would ever bring her family back.

What happened this morning, however, was another matter altogether.

"Merciful heaven," Kelly muttered, reaching for the loofah and sudsing her body so hard she left it tingling. Then, deciding she couldn't change the morning's embarrassment no matter how much she might want to, she got out of the tub and dried off.

Later, wrapped in a warm robe, she sat on the sofa close to the fireplace. Even though it was relatively early, she should try to get some sleep, but she knew any attempt to do so would be futile. Her mind was still too revved up. Besides, at home she hardly ever went to bed before midnight, usually kept company by a ton of work she brought home from the office.

Thinking about work, Kelly felt her heart falter.

She missed her office, her clients, her condo. She missed them with a passion. In the Houston Galleria area she heard the sounds of traffic, not owls. She shivered and wrapped her robe tighter around her. Something hot to drink always seemed to soothe her. Not this evening, however. Although she had made a cup of her favorite flavored coffee and took several sips of it, she still felt unsettled.

She lay back and closed her eyes, only to find the image

of Grant Wilcox unexpectedly imprinted on the back of her lids. Instead of freaking out, she let her mind have free reign—first, picturing him again in his flannel shirt and tight, faded jeans, covering a body most men would die for, then wondering what made him tick.

Why did she care?

So he was better than average looking in his rough, sexy way—she'd already conceded that. His features were carved with decisive strokes, and he had a killer smile and dimples to go along with that amazing body.

He had that muscled, yet loose-limbed agility that most big men didn't possess. She could picture him working outdoors shirtless, mending a fence, felling timber, or doing whatever he did.

Suddenly, her mind jumped ship and she imagined him without his jeans. No underwear, either.

The image didn't stop there. Next came the vision of the two of them together, naked…

Stop it! She told herself. What had gotten into her?

She was so traumatized by her thoughts, she couldn't even open her eyes. So what? No one knew what was going on inside her head. Those erotic, mental meanderings were hers and hers alone and would bring harm to no one.

Wrong.

This was a dangerous mind game she was playing—examining her life, including her loneliness and her need to be accepted and loved. Still, the images wouldn't let go—of mouths, tongues, entwined, of kisses that sucked out the soul.

The phone proved merciful to her, ringing with a jar-ring clarity just then. Lurching up, heart palpitating and drenched in sweat, Kelly let go of a pent-up breath.

"God!" she whispered, mortified and confused. Loosening her robe, she reached for the receiver.

"Hey, kiddo, how's it going?"

Ruth again. Although Kelly didn't want to talk to her, she had no choice. Perhaps her cousin's laughter was the antidote she needed to gather her scattered wits about her.

"How was the rest of the day?"

"Are you sure you want to know?" Kelly asked, a tremor in her voice.

"Uh-oh, something happen?"

"You might say so."

"Hey, I don't like the sound of that." Ruth paused. "Okay, did the help quit?"

"No way. They love me."

"Whew. That's a relief. If you knew how hard it was for me to find those two, you'd be relieved, too."

"I am. They're great."

"So, if the place is still standing and you're selling the goods, what could be so bad?"

Kelly cleared her throat. "Do you know a farmer by the name of Grant Wilcox?"

Ruth laughed. "First off, he's no farmer. He's a forester."

"Whatever."

"They aren't the same, cousin dear."

"That's a minor point, but I'll concede."

"Girl, he's the hunk I was telling you about. Surely you figured that out."

"I guessed as much."

"So what do…did…you think?"

If only you knew. "He's okay."

"Just okay?" Ruth practically screeched. "I'm not believing you. He's had every female in the county and surrounding ones try to get him down the aisle." She paused with a laugh. "Without success, I might add."

"That's too bad. You of all people know I'm not interested in being with a farmer, for God's sake." Kelly found herself squirming on the sofa.

"Forester."

Kelly ignored that. "What he is is a country bumpkin who probably prefers to hug trees rather than women." She paused. "No offense intended."

"None taken," Ruth replied with more laughter. "I know how you feel about the country. Or should I say the woods?"

"They're one and the same to me."

"Uh, right. So back to Grant. What's up with him?"

Kelly cleared her throat one more time, then told the unvarnished truth, leaving nothing out.

Afterward, there was silence on the other end of the line, then Ruth whooped like a banshee. "Oh, my God, I wish I'd been there to see that."

"You mean you're not furious at me?" Kelly asked in surprise.

"For being clumsy as a lame duck?"

"I have no leg to stand on," Kelly said, "and no pun intended."

Ruth whooped again.

Kelly simply held her silence, confused about her cousin's reaction. "It sounds like you think he deserved what he got?"

"Not at all," Ruth said, her voice still dripping with humor. "It's just that he of all men—the county stud—got burned where it hurts most."

"Ruth! I can't believe you said that."

"Well, isn't that what you did?"

"He had on jeans, Ruth. Surely—"

"When it come to scalding liquid, jeans ain't that thick. You can bet his gonads took a hit."

"I guess they did," Kelly admitted in a meek voice.

"Let's just hope, for the sake of gals still chasing him, that his pride is just burned and not charred."

"Ruth, I'm going to strangle you when I see you."

Her cousin's giggles increased.

"You're making me feel awful."

"Honey, don't worry about it," Ruth said. "Grant's a survivor. He'll be fine. He may never come back in the shop, but hey, that's the way it goes. Other than emptying hot coffee in customers' laps, how's business?"

Later, after they had talked at length about the shop, Kelly finally made her way back into the kitchen, then heard a knock on the door. She stopped midstride, then turned around and headed back to the living room. Frowning, she opened the door, only to receive the shock of her life. Her mouth gaped open.

Grant stood on the porch with flowers in hand.

Before he said anything, she felt his gaze roam over her.

She tried to swallow, but it seemed her tongue had grown too large and was about to choke her.

"It's obvious you're not expecting company." He shifted his feet. "But may I come in, anyway?"

Three

Kelly felt her breath grow shallow. Of course he couldn't come in. There was no reason for him to be here. Certainly no reason for him to come in.

Yet she continued to stand with the door open, her common sense beginning to crack. Surely she wasn't going to give in to this insanity.

She wasn't even dressed, for heaven's sake. She had nothing on under her robe, but at least it was made of thick terry cloth, impossible to see through.

Grant cocked his head and grinned. "These flowers are sure hankering for some water. I don't know how much longer they're going to survive."

Kelly shook her head and smiled. "I noticed they are a little droopy."

"See, I knew we were bound to agree on something."

She gave him an exasperated look. "Did anyone ever tell you that you're full of it?"

"Yep," he said.

That nonchalant honesty was followed by a chuckle, a deep belly chuckle that sent Kelly's already hammering pulse skyrocketing. It amazed her that this man aroused her sexual nature where others hadn't. And not from their lack of trying, either.

Even so, she hadn't looked at men through any eyes except passive ones for a long time.

So why was *he* different?

Kelly didn't know. For more reasons than one—none of which she cared to analyze, especially with him camped on Ruth's porch as if his boots had been embedded in concrete—he frightened her.

"How 'bout I promise just to stay long enough for you to put the posies in water." It wasn't a question, though his raised eyebrows made it one.

Realizing her common sense had deserted her, Kelly stood back and gestured with her hand.

Grinning, Grant removed his hat and, in two long strides, was across the threshold. Kelly closed the door and followed him, managing to keep a safe distance between them, but giving him a once-over in the process.

Not only did he look great in another pair of faded jeans and a blue T-shirt that exactly matched his eyes, but his height and the broadness of his shoulders seemed to dwarf the room, making it much too small for both of them.

With her pulse still hammering much harder than it should have been, Kelly wanted to move farther away, but knew it wouldn't do any good. There was no place to go that would put enough space between them.

"Got a vase?" he asked, that grin still in place.

"Uh, I'm sure Ruth has one around here somewhere."

"Maybe you ought to go and look."

A short tense silence followed, before she stated, "Maybe I should."

He chuckled again. "Hey, I'm harmless. Really and truly."

Kelly raised her eyebrows and smiled. *Sure you are— like a rattlesnake on a mission.* The cure for that was to keep her wits sharpened. She reached for the flowers. "Have a seat while I look for a vase."

"Sure you don't need any help?" he asked, handing them to her.

"I'm sure," she said, with more sharpness than she intended. But jeez, this man was getting under her skin, and the worst part about it, she was giving him carte blanche to let that happen, especially when she knew he'd deliberately let his hand graze hers. Light though the touch was, it left her quivering with awareness.

She finally located a vase, filled it with water and crammed the flowers into it. She then made her way back into the living room, setting the vase on a nearby table. He was bending over the fireplace, stoking the dying embers of the fire back to life.

No question he did have one cute rear end. And right now, she was privy to staring at it without his knowledge Then, realizing what she was doing and the track her mind was taking, she shook her head violently and said, "Thanks for the flowers."

He straightened and whipped around, his gaze narrowed on her. For a long moment, their eyes met and held. Finally Grant's gaze slid away, and she breathed a sigh of relief. His being here was simply not going to work if she didn't get control of her scattered emotions. God, she was acting like a teenager in the grip of hormones, for heaven's sake.

"It's a peace offering," he said, rubbing a chin that had the beginnings of a five o'clock shadow, which only added to his attractiveness.

"If that's the case, then I should be showing up on your doorstep."

"Actually, it was just an excuse to see you again." He paused and looked directly at her. "Any problem with that?"

Yes! "You certainly don't mince words," she said, stalling for time. Now was the perfect opportunity to tell him she wasn't interested in him, or any man, for that matter. Instead, she heard herself say, "Do you want to sit down?"

"I'd like nothing better, but are you sure that's what you want?"

"No," she said in a slightly unsteady voice, "I'm not sure of anything right now."

He plopped down on the sofa and concentrated on the fire while she sat on the edge of the chair adjacent. "I didn't offer you anything to drink," she said inanely.

"A beer would be nice."

She stood. "Ruth has some in the fridge."

"I don't like to drink alone."

"I have my coffee."

His belly chuckle followed her all the way to the kitchen. With her heartbeat still out of sync, she fixed the drinks and returned to the room. Meanwhile, he'd sprawled his long lets out in front of him. Unconsciously, she eyed his powerful thighs and the bulge behind his zipper.

When she realized where she was staring, she whipped her gaze up, only to find him watching her with heat in his eyes. She took a deep breath, but it didn't help. Both her face and lungs felt scorched.

He really should go.

She eased back down in the chair and watched as he took a swig of his beer. After setting the bottle on the table beside him, he said, "What brings someone like you here?"

Kelly gave a start. "Someone like me?"

"Yeah, a real classy lady who looks and acts like a fish out of water."

"My cousin needed my help, and I came to her rescue."

"Nothing's that simple."

"Perhaps not."

He reached for his beer and took another deep swig. "But that's all you're going to tell me. Right?"

"Right," she said bluntly, though she felt a smile tug at her lips.

"So you're either carrying a lot of baggage or a lot of secrets, Kelly Baker. Which is it?"

"I'm not telling."

"If you're not willing to share, how are we going to get to know each other better?"

She didn't know if he was smiling or smirking. She suspected the latter. "Guess we're not."

"Man, you know how to pull the rug right out from under a fellow." He stood, lifting his shoulders up and down as if to stretch, before stoking the fire once again. That motion called attention to his sexual agility and charisma once again. God, the man just oozed it.

"You know the fact that you will barely talk to me makes me more curious than ever," he said.

The tension heightened.

"You know what they say about curiosity." She interlaced her fingers.

"Yeah, it killed the cat." He grinned and the atmosphere eased.

"So what about you?" she asked, watching him plop back down on the sofa.

"What about me?"

"I bet you're not willing to open your life to a stranger."

He shrugged. "What do you want to know?"

She started to say, *everything,* then caught herself. "Whatever you're comfortable telling me."

"Hell, if I have anything to hide, I don't know it."

"Everyone has secrets, Mr. Wilcox."

His features turned grim. "Mr. Wilcox? You gotta be kidding me."

Her face burned. "I don't know you well enough to be on a first-name basis."

"Bullshit. The fact that you got me hot the first time I saw you puts us on familiar territory."

"Funny," Kelly retorted, though she knew her face was beet-red.

The lines around his mouth deepened, suggesting he was about to grin. "All right, Grant," she said.

"Ah, now that's better." He polished off his beer, then got back on the subject. "I guess the most important thing about me is that I have trouble staying in one place."

"Why is that?"

"Army brat. My dad was constantly on the move, so we didn't stay in one place long enough to put down roots and form long-lasting relationships.

"Are you an only child?"

"Yep. Both my parents are dead."

"Mine, too."

"Ah, be careful now, or you'll tell me something personal."

She glared at him and he laughed; then continued, "It was only when I attended Texas A & M University that I learned what settling down meant. That was tough for a roamer like me, until I met my best friend, Toby Keathly.

"Toby was majoring in forestry at A & M, and since I also loved being outside, we bonded. I ended up majoring in forestry myself and spent all the time I could with Toby in East Texas, where he grew up.

"With the money I had inherited from my parents, after graduation I purchased several hundred acres in Lane County and built the log cabin where I now live. Soon after that, I formed my own company, and traveled around the world. And now, with the signing of this new contract for cutting timber, I'm as content as a pig can be."

"That's quite a story," Kelly said.

"It's my boring life in a nutshell."

She laughed without humor. "There's nothing boring about you."

"Coming from you, I'll take that as a compliment."

"There's one thing you left out."

"Oh?"

"Your personal life. Women."

"Not much to tell there, either. What experience I've had with them taught me one important thing."

"And what was that?"

"They like men who can offer them security—home,

family, steady job, the whole package—a package that's as foreign to me as some of the countries in which I've lived."

"Do you really believe that?" He sounded like a throwback from the 1950s.

He paused and gave her a look. "Now you're meddling."

"Ah, so when push comes to shove, I'm not the only one with secrets, or is it baggage?"

"Touché!"

That word was followed by an awkward silence, then he rose. "Guess I'd better be going. It's getting late."

She didn't argue, although she experienced a twinge of disappointment she couldn't believe she was feeling about this impossible man.

"Thanks for the beer," he said at the door, turning to face her.

"Thanks for the flowers."

"Wilted and all, huh?"

He was so close now that his smell assaulted her like a blow to the stomach, especially when she noticed that his blue eyes were centered near her chest. She glanced down and saw that her robe had parted.

Before she could catch her next breath or move, the tip of his finger was trailing down her neck, her shoulder, not stopping until he had grazed the exposed side of her breast. Her mind screamed at her to push him away, but she couldn't. She flinched, not from embarrassment but from the lust that stampeded through her, holding her rooted to the spot.

His eyes darkened as he leaned toward her. In that second she sensed he was going to kiss her, and she was powerless to stop him. He moaned, then crushed his lips against hers; she sagged into him, reveling in his mouth, which was both hungry and urgent, as though if he didn't get it all now, he wouldn't get another chance.

When they finally parted, their breathing came in rapid spurts. Her emotions, at that moment, were so raw, so terrifying, that all she could do was cling to the front of his shirt.

"I've been wanting to do that since I walked through the door of the coffee shop," he rasped.

She wanted to respond, but couldn't. She didn't know what to say.

Grant spoke again, "Look, I'm leaving now, but we'll talk later." He peered down at her with anxious, searching eyes. She seemed on the edge, and he sensed that more than his kiss had propelled her there. "You're okay, right?"

No, I'm not all right!

She swallowed, then nodded. After he had left, Kelly had no idea how long she stood in a daze before she made her way to bed, where she lay across it and sobbed her heart out.

How could she have let her guard down like that, betray her husband—the love of her life—by letting this stranger kiss her? What had come over her? She didn't want to expose her heart ever again for fear of the pain and hurt she knew it could bring. She had promised herself that. And it was so important for her to keep that promise.

The sad part was she didn't know how to right the wrong she had just committed.

Grant had just finished chopping and stacking more wood that he didn't need. But who cared? If swinging an ax made him feel good and kept his frustrations at bay, then that was a-okay.

Unfortunately, his manual labor had not worked out as planned. He couldn't get Kelly off his mind even though he hadn't seen her in two days. He could still smell and feel her soft skin, as if his flesh had absorbed hers. Actually, he could damn near taste it.

That type of thinking could get a man in big trouble, because it had to do with dependency, need and becoming emotionally connected to a woman he barely knew. With Kelly Baker that was out of the question. She wasn't going to be around for long, it seemed, and he could tell she had too damn many secrets.

Still, that one kiss had turned him inside out, made him feel higher than a kite. Who was he kidding? It had made him want more. He couldn't get her breasts off his mind. Even though he'd only managed to peek at the side of one and barely touch it, he knew it would be as firm and delicious as a newly ripened peach.

Just thinking about tasting that white flesh made his mouth water.

Careful, man, he told himself. You'd best put the brakes on or you'll scare her off for sure. If he ever expected to see her again he'd have to take it easy, use finesse. Even then, she wouldn't be a pushover.

Yet he'd seen the desire in her eyes, felt the heat radiate from her body. She wanted him, too, only she might not want to admit it. Therein lay the problem. But he had no intention of giving up. If he weren't mistaken, underneath that veneer of ice was a hot, explosive woman.

While she was here, why not test the waters and find out?

With that question weighing heavily on his mind, he cleaned up his mess, then made his way into the cabin, where he showered, dressed, then grabbed a beer. The bottle was halfway to his mouth when he heard a loud rap on the door. "It's open," Grant called out.

Seconds later, his foreman and friend, Pete Akers, entered, his weathered face all grins.

"Wanna beer?" Grant asked without preamble.

Pete's grin spread as he quickened his pace. "Thought you'd never ask."

Once the foreman had his beverage in hand, they made their way back into the great room and sat near the roaring fire.

"Damn, but it's colder than Montana out there."

"How would you know?" Grant asked, giving Pete a sideways glance. "You haven't ever been out of East Texas, much less to Montana."

"Makes no difference." Pete's tone was obstinate. "I know cold when I feel it."

"Then get your bald head over here by the fire."

Once Pete had done just that and sat down, they quietly sipped their beers, both content with their own thoughts.

"What's with all that wood?" Pete finally asked. "Looks like you cut enough wood for an Alaskan winter. And here it is nearly March."

"So you noticed?"

Pete quirked a thin brow and gave Grant a penetrating look. "How could I not?"

Grant shrugged. "Guess I just needed to work off some excess energy."

This time both of Pete's brows went up. "Surely you're not stressed about anything, not when things are all going your way."

"Can't argue about that." He wasn't about to mention his fixation with the new woman in town, so he stuck to business. "Buying that tract is something I never thought would happen. And I think it'll pay off handsomely."

"Put your company on the map is the way I see it," Pete commented.

"Hopefully. In the meantime, I got a whopping lot of bills to pay at the bank. Don't forget that. As you know, the timber wasn't cheap—neither was that new equipment I had to buy."

Pete blew out his breath. "I know. When you put things in perspective, I guess you've got a helluva good reason to be stressed."

"*Stressed* is probably the wrong word," Grant admitted with a frown. "Actually, I'm excited and confident that this tract will turn a profit and get me out of debt. So update me." He set his empty bottle down and gave his foreman a straight look.

"I've already placed both crews."

"Equipment and all?"

"Yep," Pete said in an animated voice, as though proud of that accomplishment.

"Have you found another foreman?"

Pete frowned. "I thought maybe you and me together could handle it. You know how I am about hiring people I don't know."

"But you know everyone around these parts."

"That's why I ain't hiring nobody." Peter cocked his head. "Get my drift?"

"That'll work, especially since none of the other tracts are cuttable right now due to the poor conditions."

"Let's hope the rain continues to hold off."

"It will. I'm convinced my luck has changed and all for the better. So where did you put the log sets?" Grant asked, back to business.

"I put one crew on the northwest side next to the county road and the other on the south end next to the old home place."

"I'll work the south end," Grant said, knowing it would be the most difficult site to cut.

"The saw heads are already buzzing and it looks like we're going to be able to get twelve to fourteen loads per day."

"Man, if we do that for six weeks to two months, then I'd be on easy street for sure."

Grant grinned and raised his hand. Pete hit it in a high-five just as Grant's cell phone rang. Frowning, he reached for it, noticing that the call was from Dan Holland, the landowner who had sold him the timber.

"What's up, buddy?" Grant asked without mincing words.

"I'm afraid we got a problem."

Four

Did he regret the kiss?

Probably.

Kelly figured that was the reason she hadn't seen him today. Of course, she didn't know for a fact. As always, her mind was her own worst enemy, taking off like a runaway train, imagining all sorts of crazy things.

Since she'd been in charge of the shop, she'd seen Grant only *once*. He hadn't been a regular customer so why would he stop in again?

The truth was, she couldn't stop thinking about the kiss. If only she hadn't let that happen, she'd be just fine. But she'd made an unwise choice, and choices had consequences. She wanted to see him again, even though she kept reminding herself that would be foolish.

Kelly's life was back in Houston. She would soon be

gone from Lane, Texas. More to the point, she couldn't wait to get back to her *real* job, and to the challenge it offered.

"Kelly, phone for you."

Jerking her mind back to reality, she smiled at Albert, went into the small office and picked up the receiver. It was her boss, John Billingsly.

"How's it going?" he asked in a pleasant tone.

"Do you really want to know?" Though she had a deep respect for John and thought of him as a friend as well as a boss, he wasn't exactly high on her fan list now. After all, if it weren't for him, she wouldn't be stuck here.

His sigh filtered through the line. "You know I do, or I wouldn't have asked."

"Actually, things are going better than I thought they would down here, though I hate to admit that."

He chuckled. "I know you're still unhappy with me."

"And will be for a long time." Although Kelly had spoken bluntly and truthfully, there was no rancor in her words.

"You know how much I care about you, Kelly. I only want what's best for you."

"I know." And she did. At times she sensed he would like to be more than her boss, yet he'd never once crossed that professional line. She thought there was more to his feelings than he had ever expressed, however.

"So just stay put for a while longer," John said, "to give your body and mind a chance to completely heal. That's all I'm asking."

"Do I have a choice?"

"No," he said in a soft but firm tone.

She knew he was right, though she was loath to admit

that. Both John and Dr. Rivers, her psychiatrist, had told her that, but it was John who had made a believer out of her. He hadn't exactly threatened the security of her job, but he had certainly threatened her pending promotion, a position she wanted badly.

She remembered that day so well. He had called her into his corner office. When she'd taken a seat, John had gotten up, come around his desk, sat in the chair closest to her and taken her hand. "Look me in the eye and tell me you're not struggling?"

Kelly couldn't. Tears clogged her vision as her shoulders began to shake. "Have I hurt the firm? If I have, I'm so sorry."

"I won't lie and say you haven't made some bad decisions and choices recently, because you have. But I think you know that yourself. You haven't damaged the firm— not yet. That's what we're trying to avoid."

"Thank God." Kelly had hung on to his hand and squeezed it.

"You have a chance to become a partner in this firm," John said, "but only if you get control of your emotions and become the attorney we know you can be."

But that's the person I was before my daughter and husband were killed by a drunk driver, she'd wanted to scream.

As if John had read her thoughts, he'd added, "You have to come to grips with your loss."

"I have," Kelly cried, jerking her hand out of his. She resented being patronized, as if she was a child. She dug her fingers into her palms. She couldn't believe this. She was Kelly Baker, firm overachiever. She had brought into the firm some of its biggest and best clients. Shouldn't that count for something? Apparently not, because at the first sign of trouble they wanted to toss her away like a piece of garbage.

Her conscience suddenly rebelled, reminding her that she was blowing John's words way out of proportion. Deep down, she knew he and the company were firmly on her side.

"No, you haven't faced your loss," he said softly, patiently. "Far from it, and that's the problem. You've buried your pain and heartache in your work. Now, four years after the fact, the headache you never faced, or dealt with openly, is doing a number on you. It's taking its toll on your emotions and your health. We both know you're on the brink of having a complete breakdown."

She hated to admit that he was right, but he was.

Push had come to shove and she could no longer fool herself into thinking she and everything around her was just fine.

"I know your cousin needs help, Kelly," John said into the growing silence. "Go and help her. New surroundings, new people, new job…" He paused with a lopsided smile. "Although I can't imagine you serving coffee or food, you'll give it you all, like you do everything else you tackle."

She forced a smile. "I can't imagine that either, but it looks like you've given me no choice."

"That's right," John admitted in a stern voice.

Because her throat was too full to speak, Kelly had leaned over and kissed him on the cheek, then walked out. That had been three weeks ago. Three of the longest weeks of her life.

"Kelly, are you still there?" John asked into the silence now.

"Yes. Sorry. Actually, I was just rehashing our last conversation."

"That's good, because nothing has changed on this end."

"I know." She heard the break in her voice but hoped he hadn't. She wanted to keep her dignity at all costs.

"You get back to work. I'll talk to you again soon."

The second she replaced the receiver and walked back into the dining area, Kelly pulled up short. Grant was walking in the door with a scowl on his face.

Her heart dropped to her toes. She'd been right; he wasn't glad to see her. Then why was he here? Simple. He wanted some food or coffee. Maybe both.

"You look surprised to see me," he said in a pleasant enough tone, however, his big body striding toward a table.

Today he was dressed a little more formally than he had been before. He had on jeans and boots, of course, but his shirt was smooth cotton, not flannel, and instead of his hard hat, he had on a black Stetson, which he removed.

"Actually, I am," Kelly said with honesty once she found her tongue. After that she didn't know what to say, which was totally unlike her. But then she reminded herself she'd just recently kissed this man's mouth with hot, heady passion, which had and still did unnerve her to the core.

When he'd walked by her, she'd gotten a whiff of his scent—fresh and good, as if he'd just gotten out of the shower. That added to her unnerved state.

Feeling her face flame, Kelly turned away. She hadn't had thoughts like that since her husband died. "Would you care for something to drink?" she finally asked. "Or eat?"

"Coffee'll do."

"Are you sure you want me to serve it?" She made herself ask that with a smile hoping to lighten his mood. Probably another foolish move.

The scowl on his face softened and he actually grinned, which affected her heart again. God, she had to get hold of herself.

"Sure, though notice I'm sitting real close to the table." She smiled again.

This time he didn't reciprocate. That scowl reappeared, even fiercer than before.

Feeling as though she were treading in deep water, Kelly got his coffee and carefully placed the mug in front of him. "You seem upset." A flat statement of act. If it had to do with her, she wanted to know it.

"Yeah, but not at you." His eyes met hers.

She felt a flush steal into her face.

He leaned forward and said in a low, husky voice, "You look so damn good, if I had my way, I'd grab you right now and kiss you until you begged me to stop. Even then, I'm not sure I would."

His provocative statement took her aback so much that all she could do was stand there speechless while a flush of heat charged through her body.

"Do you have a minute?"

"Sure," she said, uneasy that she was going to hear something she didn't want to.

He pulled out the chair adjacent to him and indicated that she sit.

"Let me get a cup of coffee first. I'll be right back." Once she'd returned and sat down, they remained silent while taking several sips out of the big mugs. Finally she said, "Something's happened."

Grant's brows bunched together and he sighed. "You got that right."

"Want to talk about it?"

"I'm looking for a good attorney. Know any?"

Kelly's heart skipped a beat, but she kept her calm facade in place. *Did she ever!* "With all your business dealings, I'm surprised you don't have one."

"I do, but unfortunately he's out of the country. And his partner's an idiot."

Kelly's eyebrows rose, but she simply said, "Okay."

"Sorry. That's not exactly true. Let's just say we don't see eye to eye on things."

Kelly merely nodded, then asked, "Why do you think you need an attorney?" If he didn't want to tell her, he didn't have to, but apparently he wanted someone to talk to or he wouldn't have said anything to begin with.

"Dan Holland, the landowner I bought the timber from, just called me and dropped a friggin' bombshell."

"Oh?"

"Yeah, and one of the worst things about it is that I thought he was my friend."

"Friendship and business are two different things, Grant. You should know that."

"I do know that, dammit. Still, in a small town, a man's word is as good as his signature. And I had both from Dan."

"So what's changed?" Kelly pressed, sensing his tempter building to no good end.

"He wants my crews to stop cutting timber."

"And the reason?"

"Some crap about an illegitimate half brother showing up out of the blue and wanting a say in the deal Dan and his brothers had just made with me."

Kelly was not only shocked but puzzled. "And your friend's buying that story and wants to stop the deal?"

"Hook, line and sinker. He said that if Larry Ross—that's the guy's name—turns out to be legit, then he has a right to be included."

"Sounds ludicrous."

"It's more than that. It's crazy as hell."

"So what was your response?" Kelly asked.

"I told Holland he was nuts if he let some bozo he's never seen before waltz in and make that kind of claim, and not tell him to take a freakin' hike."

"I find it unbelievable that he didn't," Kelly said, shaking her head in dismay.

"Dan said he'd never seen me this upset."

Kelly's eyes widened. "I have a feeling that was the wrong thing to say."

"You're right. I told him if he thought I was upset now, just wait. He ain't seen nothing yet. At the moment, I was as calm as the Pope taking a nap."

Kelly shook her head. "What a mess."

"There's more," Grant said. "Dan defended this Ross character, saying that his dad had been a womanizer, that it was possible he'd had an affair and Larry Ross could be the product of that affair.

"And apparently the woman, Ross's mother, said that she'd kept quiet long enough, swearing to her son that Lucas Holland was definitely Ross's daddy and that Ross should get anything and everything that was entitled to him."

Kelly gave him a pointed look. "And your response?"

"Hogwash."

Her lips twitched.

Grant blew out a long breath. "I told him that's just too pat, too hokey. Ross is his problem, not mine. And if he is legit or not has zip to do with me. We have a deal that is on the up-and-up—signed, sealed and delivered."

"He didn't see it that way, right?"

"You got it. Apparently Larry Ross has threatened to file an injunction to stop my operation, claiming his family doesn't have the right to sell the timber without his signature."

Kelly was aghast and it showed.

"This is crazy, because at the time Dan didn't even know this guy existed. But this Ross character evidently doesn't care.

"So I told Holland to give me my money back. An injunction could wipe me out financially."

"What was his response?" Kelly asked, becoming more appalled by the second. She felt her brain churning as it hadn't in three weeks. Grant was right. He needed an attorney ASAP.

"He said he couldn't do it, that his brothers had left it up to him to do the investing, and he'd put all the money in non-liquid assets."

"That man's a piece of work."

"I said that's your problem, not mine. Of course Dan whined that we could work something out, that all he's asking of me was to suspend operations for several days until this mess could be straightened out."

"I hope you told him sorry, no can do."

"That's exactly what I told him. His comeback was that I was being unreasonable. So I asked him what if the shoe were on the other foot? Would he be so eager to give in? His answer was no, so I told him the simple solution was to borrow the money against his assets and pay the creep off."

"If he'd gone for that," Kelly said, "we wouldn't be having this conversation.

"Right again," Grant stated. "You know, Kelly, friend or no friend, a deal's a deal. I kept my end of the bargain, and I expect him to keep his. Dan got pissed and assured me I hadn't heard the end of this.

"If it's a fight he wants, then, by God, that's what he's gonna get. I *will* cut *my* timber."

"Maybe I can help."

Grant looked startled. "You?"

"That's what I said." Kelly kept her tone low and even.

He laughed. "How? Use your waitress skills and dump hot coffee in his lap?"

Kelly knew he was trying to be funny. But to her, his comment was anything but that. Forcing a sugary smile, she stood and said, "I agree that my waitress skills are lacking. But when I'm practicing law, I'm a damn good attorney."

Grant went pale, as if she'd just cut his throat.

"*You're* an attorney?" His laughter rang through the shop.

Five

He should've kept his mouth shut. Laughing at Kelly hadn't been smart, especially when he was backed into a corner and she had offered to help. But the thought of her being an attorney had never occurred to him. He'd just thought she was a pretty shoulder to cry on.

Kelly Baker, Esquire. It was hard for him to grasp that.

Grant slapped his forehead and cursed, calling himself every derogatory term he could think of and more. But kicking his backside after the fact didn't do any good. The only way to right this wrong was to tuck his tail between his legs and get down on bended knee. That thought made his eyebrows shoot up. Wouldn't that be a sight to behold, him on his knees in front of a woman?

At this point, he was ready to do whatever it took to get him out of this mess. But it wouldn't be easy. He'd almost rather face a grizzly than Kelly; probably have a better chance of winning.

He compressed his lips. He'd been tempted to call Ruth and find out what type of attorney Kelly was.

Then he'd decided that might set off another kind of fire he didn't want any part of. Ruth might think he had an ulterior motive, like a personal interest in Kelly or something, which couldn't be further from the truth.

Liar.

Grant winced. His conscience was at work again, pricking him, keeping him on the straight and narrow. He'd kissed her, dammit. But that was as far, and as personal, as things had gone. Which was not to say he didn't want more, he did.

Her breasts. They were driving him wild. What little he'd seen of them made him want much more.

"Dammit, Wilcox," he muttered tersely. He had to delete those erotic thoughts of her from his mind, or they would cripple him businesswise. Perhaps it had been too long since he'd been with woman. But everything about Kelly made him like he hadn't in eons.

But to get involved with her in any way would be like sticking his hand in a hornet's nest, expecting to get badly stung.

Still, if Kelly were truly a lawyer—and people didn't lie about things like that—he'd screwed up by laughing at her. He gritted his teeth and fisted his hands in disgust.

He should've known there was more to her than met the eye. Right off, he'd figured her for a classy lady. And when she'd refused to tell him anything about herself, he'd picked up on the fact that she had too damn many secrets. He just hadn't guessed *that* one.

Solution?

Suck up to Kelly big time.

Unfortunately, she didn't appear to be the type where groveling would work. Still, he had to try. What did he have to lose? He smiled.

He knew she wasn't indifferent to him. Their wanting each other had been mutual; he'd swear to that. Like magnets, they had been drawn to one another. And that kiss—God, when he'd put his hot, open mouth on hers…

Enough, Wilcox, he told himself, getting up from his desk and heading to the kitchen. He'd spent far too much energy on Kelly Baker. She'd either help him or she wouldn't.

Grant peered at his watch, then groaned. He'd lollygagged around the house for far too long. He should already be at the site. No. He should be at Kelly's.

He grabbed his hat just as his cell rang.

"Where are you?" Pete asked.

From the sound of his foreman's voice, Grant knew something was amiss. "At home."

"You'd best get your ass here pronto."

Grant's stomach clenched. "What's going on?"

There was silence for a moment, then his foreman stated, "Just get here."

Thirty minutes later, Grant whipped his truck into his usual parking spot at the edge of the log set and knew immediately what had Pete in such a dither. The sheriff's car was parked in front of one of the large pieces of equipment. The crew was huddled close by, talking quietly among themselves.

Pete looked as if he was about to punch Sheriff Sayers in the nose.

"Good morning, Amos," Grant said calmly, after easing out of his truck and striding toward the two men, determined to diffuse the highly charged situation.

Amos Sayers was a tall string bean of a man with glasses and big ears.

"Good morning, sir," Amos responded, with an obvious change in tone and attitude following Grant's arrival.

After handshakes, a short, uncomfortable silence ensued. Amos was the first to break it. "You're going to have to shut down."

"I haven't seen anything in writing," Grant said with a show of self-confidence.

Amos slapped a piece of paper into Grant's hand. "Well, you have now."

He didn't even bother to look it. "You're really shutting me down?"

"I don't have any choice." Amos's booted foot pawed the dirt. "I'm just carrying out the judge's order."

"So you are."

"Then you're going to comply with the injunction?" Amos asked, his tone unsure. "And suspend operations?"

A shocked-looking Pete muttered, "I hope to hell you're not going to let this young whippersnapper here dictate to us."

"You want to go to jail?" Amos demanded, his confidence blooming.

Pete shook his head violently.

"Didn't think so."

Amos pawed the dirt once more, then looked straight at

Grant. "Again, I'm sorry about all this, sir." Then he walked back to his car and got in.

"What are you going to do?" The foreman asked in a bleak tone.

"Get a lawyer and get us working again."

"What about the one you've used for years?"

"He's out of the country."

"Got another one in mind?" Pete asked.

"Yep."

Pete gave him a strange look, then said flatly, "You'll call me?"

"As soon as I know something."

Pressing his mouth into a thin line, Grant jumped back in his truck and drove off. He knew what he had to do, but he damn sure didn't have to like it.

Would this day ever end? Kelly asked herself. It was only ten o'clock on Monday morning and she was bored out of her mind. Yesterday hadn't been too bad because she'd been so tired. She had stayed in her lounging pj's most of the day, dozing off and on between reading a murder mystery and watching television.

Today, however, was a different story. She wished the shop wasn't closed on Mondays. One day off in this hole-in-the-wall town was enough. Two in a row was more than she could take.

More depressed than ever, Kelly walked to the window and stared out at the cold, cloudy world. It seemed there was more gloomy weather lately than sunny. But then it was late February, she reminded herself. It wasn't supposed to be warm and uplifting.

Yet in Texas, it could easily have been a beautiful eighty degrees on this very day. Sighing, she turned from the window, walked back to the chair and sat down, pulling her legs under her. After staring blankly at the wall for a while, she reached for her purse nearby, pulled out her wallet and watched it fall open to her pictures.

Her husband's was the first one she saw. Eddie truly had been tall, dark and handsome. More than that, he'd been a sweet, gentle man who had adored her and their daughter, Amber.

Even though Kelly stared at his face now as she had in person so many times in the past, it was hard to remember how it had felt when he'd touched her. She knew she had loved him profoundly at one time, but she couldn't remember what that was like, either. Everything about him had faded with time.

Not so with her daughter. As she looked at her picture, a piercing pain robbed Kelly of her next breath. Her precious baby. Her beautiful child. Her Amber, with her small face smiling up at her. Knowing that she would never see her again, never touch her again—even after four years—was unthinkable.

Unbearable.

Yet the finality of leaving her child in the cold, dark ground was the reality that had finally caught up with Kelly and driven her close to the edge of insanity.

Taking a deep, shuddering breath, she forced a smile through the tears now streaming down her face. She remembered so well the very day that picture had been taken. Amber had just turned three and she'd gotten that dress for her birthday. It was pink and frilly and girlie, just like

Amber. Even though she had bright red curls all over her head, the pink was perfect on her.

Kelly had nestled a pink bow among those curls, but it hadn't been easy. "Be still, squirt blossom," she had told her squirming daughter. "It'll only take a second."

That had been true. The second Amber had scrambled off her lap, she had jerked the ribbon out.

"You little toot, you," Kelly had said, scooping her up, positioning her on her lap and going through the process one more time.

That time the ribbon had stayed put, but only because Kelly had promised Amber an ice cream cone if she'd leave it in. Even at three, her child was smart enough to know a bribe when she heard one, and was smart enough to hold Kelly to it.

Amber had demanded two cones, though in a sweet voice and with her beautiful smile.

If Amber had lived, she would have been as lovely on the inside as she'd been on the outside. She'd had her father's gentle nature. When Amber looked at anyone with those big, dark brown eyes, their hearts had melted into a puddle.

Suddenly a sob caught in Kelly's throat and she slammed the wallet shut. She raised her head determined not to drown in her tears, then stood up. She hadn't had a spell of self-pity like this in quite some time. Homesickness and boredom were to blame, she told herself. Being all alone.

And Grant Wilcox with his condescension and dismissal. She couldn't leave him out.

She had composed herself and wiped the tears from her face when she heard a knock. "Oh, brother," she muttered, wondering who it was.

Kelly opened the door and felt her mouth go slack. Grant Wilcox stood squarely in front of her.

"I know the shop's closed," he said in a sheepish tone, "but I thought you might serve some crow here. Is that true?"

Six

Kelly was mystified that Grant had sought her out away from the shop again. He actually seemed embarrassed, a state that didn't fit with this forester and his killer dimples.

When he'd kissed her that night, she had noticed those tantalizing dents in his cheeks. Thank goodness she had managed to put them out of her mind. She didn't care about Grant Wilcox, she reminded herself quickly. He'd insulted her. Today of all days, she wasn't in the forgiving mood, which she saw as a good thing. This man was obnoxious, sexist—and had gotten too far under her skin.

To her dismay, he remained there.

Standing in front of her, propping his shoulder against the door post, he looked hot. And lethal. His hair, a bit shaggy for her taste, looked as freshly laundered as he did, dressed in jeans that adhered to his body in all the right places, a white shirt that flattered his dark blue eyes, and boots that made him seem taller and more brawny than usual.

She had to admit, whether she'd first thought he was Farmer Brown or not, he was one fine specimen.

Go figure.

Feeling unwanted color creep into her cheeks, Kelly turned slightly, hoping he wouldn't see her reaction to her thoughts. And the idea he might read them was more mind-boggling.

"Is the inside off-limits?" he asked in his deep sexy voice, putting an end to the silence.

"That depends."

"On what?" he asked.

"I haven't decided yet."

"I can handle that."

"Actually, I'm thinking," she said in a slightly husky tone before clearing her throat.

Although a tentative smile teased his lips, Grant refrained from saying anything that might shatter the fragile truce between them. Smart fellow, Kelly thought, One stray word, and she would've sent him away without a qualm.

"I guess it's okay for you to come in," she finally said with a sigh.

As before, once he had crossed the threshold into Ruth's small living room, everything seemed to shrink. His body warmth was something Kelly had hoped to avoid, but she couldn't. He crowded her.

He was just a big man, something she wasn't used to, she reminded herself. It was no big deal—if she didn't make it one. Eddie had been of much smaller stature.

"You didn't answer my question," Grant said, remaining on his feet.

Since she'd asked him in, her manners rose to the surface. "If you'd like, you can sit down."

He gave a shrug, then said, "Thanks. Don't mind if I do."

Kelly remained standing, thinking that gave her some leverage, which was ludicrous, she knew. No matter: she wasn't ready to sit and welcome him as an invited guest. Not yet, anyway.

"You still haven't answered my question," he pressed.

"That's because I don't recall it."

She wasn't fibbing either, not entirely. Seeing him at her door had been such a shock that what he'd said had flown right out of her mind.

"I asked if you were serving crow?"

Despite herself, Kelly felt her lips relax into a smile. "We definitely have it on the menu at the shop."

"For jerks like me, huh?"

"If the shoe fits…" Again she found herself smiling, then forced herself to grow sober. She didn't intend to cut this roughneck any slack. Although he hadn't offended her as much as she'd pretended, her reaction had put much-needed space between them. She thought about him too much for her peace of mind.

"In my case, the shoe definitely fits. And snugly, too."

"If you say so." His apology made no difference. She had no intention of rescuing him. There were plenty of lawyers in this area as competent as her—more so, probably.

Besides, the less she had to do with this man, the better. She must've had temporary mind loss to have offered to help him in the first place, especially when work was the last thing she was supposed to be thinking about.

"Will you accept my apology?" he prodded, appearing

to have hunkered down comfortably in the sofa close to the roaring fire, which gave the room a cozy feel.

Kelly shrugged. "Okay, apology accepted."

She saw his mouth tense, but only for a second, then it went slack and a sheepish look stole over his face. "Something tells me my apology fell far short of its target." His eyes delved into hers.

Rebelling against that magnetic pull, she stiffened. "Hey, give it a rest. You've apologized and I've accepted. The end."

Grant rubbed his chin. "That's what I'm afraid of, which means I'm going to have to do some major kissing up."

"Why would you even bother?" Kelly asked, remaining upright, suddenly tired of this conversation. Elements of her Houston lawyer persona were returning. She knew she should be hospitable and offer him something to drink, but if she did, that might mean he'd hang around. Even though she was definitely lonely and feeling sorry for herself, this man was hardly the one she'd choose to comfort her.

Heaven forbid.

"I have to have an attorney."

"But not me."

"Yes, you."

"How can you be so sure of that?"

"Because you're the most accessible," he said without hesitation. "And I need—*needed*—legal counsel yesterday."

"If nothing else, at least you're honest."

"So what do you say?"

"You don't even know what kind of law I practice."

"Does it matter?"

"Sure, it does. For all you know, I might be just a tax lawyer."

"Are you?"

"No."

Grant spread his hands. "Enough said."

Suddenly irritated at him and his reasoning, Kelly shook her head. "I'm not supposed to be working."

A puzzled look came over his face. "Why? You get disbarred or something?"

"No, I didn't get disbarred or something," she said with forced patience."

As if he realized he'd once again opened his mouth and inserted his big foot, he said in a sincere tone, "Look, I'm sorry. But there's something about you—" He broke off abruptly, as if he feared eating more of that shoe leather.

Kelly had no qualms about finishing the sentence. "That makes *you* say and do things you otherwise wouldn't say or do?"

"Yeah. How did you know?"

"Maybe I feel the same way."

The fact that she admitted that tidbit seemed to shock him. It shocked her, too, actually. The less personal she kept things between them the better off she would be. In fact, the sooner she got rid of him, the better.

"I'll beg if I have to," he said, peering at the fire, then back at her.

His eyes were narrowed and unreadable, but she sensed a desperation in his big body she hadn't noted before. He probably thought that if he apologized, she'd capitulate.

He was wrong. One more time.

"Begging's off-limits here."

He smiled wryly. "How about kneeling?"

She kept a straight face, but it was hard. "That's off-limits, as well."

"You don't cut a man much slack do you?"

"Only if he deserves it."

Color slowly drained from his face. "I was an ass. I've already admitted that. But if you really can't help me, then I'll leave and not bother you again."

Suddenly Kelly felt guilty. Why was that? Perhaps deep down she was dying to do something, *anything*, that pertained to law. And fighting an injunction would be simple compared to what she was used to—at least if the judge was not some old crusty curmudgeon who thought he was God in this neck of the woods.

She wouldn't be surprised if that was the case. If so, then she would be dead in the water as far as wielding any influence. Country and city lawyers mixed like oil and water. Still, she yearned to give the case a shot. Anything other that serving pie and coffee.

"The fact you haven't kicked me out yet gives me hope."

She heard a touch of little-boy eagerness in Grant's tone and it got to her. Dammit, *he* got to her. If only he wouldn't look at her like that. And even though she couldn't define what she meant by *that*, she recognized desire in a man when she saw it. And though that made her uncomfortable, it also made her feel like a woman for the first time in a long while.

"Would you care for something to drink?"

Grant's head popped back up. She'd surprised him again. Good. He didn't need to be sure of her. Then she chastised herself for caring what other women thought about him.

"Still have some beer?"

"I think so."

"It's okay if you don't."

"I'll see."

A few minutes later she returned with two opened bottles of beer. Although it was obviously Ruth's choice of drink, Kelly could barely tolerate the stuff. But today, she decided to join him.

They sipped in silence for a few minutes. Surprisingly, Kelly felt herself relax. Until now, her nerves were all twisted inside. She attributed that change to the beer, even though she'd only had two sips. Still, it didn't take much for her to feel its effects. That was why she seldom drank. With that thought, she set her bottle on the table in front of her and watched as he tossed his head back and chugged down half of his at one time.

Maybe he wasn't as comfortable or sure of himself as he'd like her to think.

"I've been shut down."

Kelly blinked. "Pardon?"

Grant blew out a breath, then finished his beer. "To put it in simple terms, my crews are not allowed to cut the timber I bought."

"So that guy did get an injunction?"

"Yep."

"Have you spoken to him yourself?"

"Not yet. Right now, I probably need to stay as far away from him as possible in order not to rip his head off his shoulders."

"I'd say that's smart." Kelly couldn't keep her sarcasm at bay, though she didn't doubt for a moment that Grant

Wilcox was serious and capable of doing exactly what he set out to do—even if he had to harm another person.

She shuddered inwardly. What was she considering getting herself into?

"So are you going to help me?" Grant had straightened and moved his big body closer to the edge of the sofa.

She sat across from him and held her silence, all the while gnawing on the inside of her lip. She knew she'd regret what she was about to do, but she was going to do it anyway. But not for him, she told herself. Her efforts were purely self-serving.

Regardless of what her doctor said, she needed a challenge or she would wither and die, even though her time here was short-lived. Serving food and beverages was simply not cutting it. Hadn't that recent crying jag proved that?

"I'm making no promises, understand," Kelly said at length, "but I will advise you on what legal advice you need."

Grant blew out a relieved breath. "Thank God."

"Don't be thanking him yet. And certainly not me."

"Uh, right."

"You'll have to indulge me. I'm a good attorney, but I'm not familiar with the timber industry or anything pertaining to it. I just know that trees are cut in the woods and used for a lot of things—building homes, paper products." She paused with a slight grin. "Including toilet paper."

He laughed, then explained in careful detail a little of how his industry worked and his part in the process. "I find landowners willing to sell some of their timber. I buy those standing trees, cut them, then sort them by size and quality.

Once that's done, the wood is hauled to contracted mills, where they're processed and shipped worldwide."

"So unless you cut, the company loses—big."

"I am the company," Grant stressed. "And as I mentioned before, this could ruin me financially."

Kelly nodded. "Go on."

"My payments on my equipment, now sitting idle in the woods, run over fifty thousand a month."

Kelly gasped.

"Oh, I haven't finished yet," Grant said. "And because I had spent my cash on tracts of timber that aren't loggable right now thanks to the wet weather, I had to borrow money to buy this large tract."

"So how much is your equipment and timber altogether?"

"Close to a hundred thou a month. So you see why I have to settle this matter now," Grant added in a harsh tone. "When my crews aren't working, I have zero dollars coming in."

"That makes sense."

"I can't let Holland *or* this Ross guy get by with this tomfoolery. If I don't get back to cutting soon—" He broke off, his features contorted.

He didn't have to finish the sentence. Owing that kind of money could be a financial death sentence for a businessman if the notes weren't paid. And that wasn't even talking about paying the bank *on time*.

"All right," she conceded, "I'll see what I can do."

He looked cautiously relieved. "You will?"

"That's what I said, but again, I'm making no promises."

"Don't worry, you'll be compensated."

"That's the least of my worries."

Grant cleared his throat, then said, "Thanks. I really appreciate you doing this."

Kelly merely nodded, and a silence fell between them.

He was the first to break it. "Do you mind me asking you something?"

"That depends."

"It has nothing to do with me."

That should've been warning enough to nip the conversation in the bud right then, but she didn't. "Ask."

"Were you crying?" Grant paused and angled his head. "You looked so incredibly sad."

Kelly stiffened, forgetting her crying jag just moments before he had knocked on her door. She was sure the remnants of it were still visible. She must look a sight— nose red and eyes all bloodshot. And some of her makeup was probably streaking her cheeks.

But what did her looks matter? She certainly wasn't trying to impress him. Not in that, way in any case..

"I was thinking about my husband and child."

He looked dumbfounded while a suffocating silence fell over the room.

Then he said, with harsh surprise, "You're *married?*"

Seven

"I'm not," she said with in a faltering voice, turning her face away from his intense, inquiring eyes.

Although he appeared more perplexed that stunned now, but he didn't say anything. Instead, he continued to stare at her. She wanted to avoid that piecing gaze at all costs, but she couldn't seem to avert her eyes.

At times it seemed that he had the power to see straight through her. No man had ever affected her that way. But again, he wasn't just any man—something she'd sensed from the first moment she'd seen him.

She had to handle this situation with the utmost care, as though she was holding the most fragile glass object. Inside, that was exactly how she felt—fragile to the breaking point.

"Kelly?"

She didn't remember him calling her by name before,

not in that low and slightly sexy voice, causing her heart to turn over. Fighting for composure, she drew a deep breath that she hoped would clear her head and get her through these next terrible moments. He wouldn't be there much longer. Then she could relax.

Or could she?

She had agreed to help get him out of his present jam, which meant she would be seeing much more of him, certainly more than she'd ever intended.

Terrific. But whose fault was that? She couldn't blame Grant. He hadn't forced her to make a commitment to help him. If the truth be known, she was thrilled that he'd asked for her advice. Not because of who he was but because she would be working, doing the thing she loved best in the world—practicing law. She couldn't believe how much the idea exited her.

"Hello?"

"Sorry," she muttered, feeling heat flood her face.

"Don't be sorry. I just didn't want you to forget I was here."

She almost laughed at that. That wasn't about to happen, not when his big body dominated the premises, and the fresh scent of his cologne drove her senses wild. But she wasn't about to tell him that or even hint at it. The sooner she got rid of him, the sooner she could collect herself.

Until the next time she saw him.

"Look, forget I mentioned your family or why you were crying. I stepped out of line. It's obviously none of my business."

Unexpectedly, and to her mortification, tears suddenly

welled up again in her eyes. This time Kelly wasn't quick enough to turn her face before he saw them.

"Hey, is there something I can do to help you?" Grant asked rather awkwardly, that sexy roughness still in his voice. "After all, you agreed to save my bacon. Maybe I could return the favor."

"I don't think so," she whispered, frantically blinking the tears from her eyes. How embarrassing to break down in front of a man who was practically a total stranger. Not only did that make her angry, it frightened her. She had come here to regain control of her emotions, to heal, so she could return to work and be the crackerjack attorney she once was.

At this rate, she was going to be in worse shape when she returned than when she left Houston. And with her once-sharp wits dulled, too.

Boredom. That was the problem. She didn't have enough to keep her mind occupied or challenged. But thanks to this man and his unfortunate business situation, now she did. Although it appeared to be a simple case, it had to do with lawyering, and she was grateful for the opportunity.

Then why wasn't she smiling instead of crying?

When she'd gathered her wits about her one more time, she found Grant's gaze still trained on her. For a second their eyes met, and to her dismay, a spark of electricity leaped between them.

Good Lord. She caught her breath and she held it for what seemed the longest time. This couldn't be happening.

She sensed he'd been zapped by that same spark and was thinking about it as he cleared his throat, then reached for his hat and made a move to leave.

The words spilled out. "My husband and child were killed in an automobile accident."

He stopped abruptly. Silence once again overtook the room.

Kelly guessed that was a good thing, because she was too flabbergasted to say anything else. She was too flabbergasted to even budge. She felt frozen inside and out. What on earth had possessed her to blurt that out? He'd already apologized for intruding in her life, which meant they had moved past her tears and he'd been getting ready to leave. Why had she said anything?

Now, she had opened that can of worms again, leaving herself totally vulnerable to him. Her eyes swept tentatively back to his. As she'd suspected, his gaze were definitely probing, his blue eyes so dark they looked black.

"That's a tough one," he finally said in a strained voice.

"Yes," she whispered, "it was. It nearly killed me—emotionally, that is."

"I'm sure it did. What happened?"

Kelly took a shaky breath. That was when Grant reached over and touched her hand, only to quickly withdraw his when the sparks once again zapped them both.

"You don't have to answer that," he stated, clearly shaken.

"It's the same story you've heard about a million times," Kelly said in a dull voice. "A drunk driver, a teenager, veered into their lane and hit them head-on. The kid was speeding and they all were killed instantly."

"God, I'm sorry."

"Me, too."

Another silence stretched.

"When did it happen?"

"Four years ago."

Grant didn't respond, but she could see the wheels turning in his mind. Like everyone else, he was thinking she should be over the tragedy by now, that she should've pulled herself and her life back together.

"I know what you're thinking," she said with strength in her voice.

Grant raised his eyebrows. "Oh? And just what would that be?"

"That I should be through wallowing in self-pity."

"Actually, I was thinking just the opposite."

She gave him a startled look.

"Yeah, I was wondering how the hell you kept your sanity and still functioned, especially as an attorney."

His answer so surprised her that her mouth dropped open. "Time," she finally said. "I didn't believe my shrink when he told me that, but I do now. Time is the greatest healer of all."

"Yet you're not completely healed."

"No, and I never will get over what happened. That's why I'm here."

"So now I know one of your secrets," he said in a gentle voice.

"Oh, I'm sure others are wondering about me, too, since I stick out like a sore thumb in the shop."

"Hey, you're doing just fine…" Grant paused, then smiled. "Except when you have a coffee cup in hand. Then you become a mite dangerous."

"A lethal weapon, right?" she added wryly.

"I can only speak for myself."

They both smiled before sobering once again.

"Was your child a boy or girl?" he asked.

"A girl. Her name is…was Amber."

"I like that."

"My husband's name was Eddie. He was an attorney also, but for another firm."

"Sounds like the perfect all-American family."

"We were," she said with another catch in her voice.

"We don't have to talk about this anymore if you don't want to. It's your call."

"My doctor says that talking is exactly what I should do. Not talking about it and pushing the pain deep down inside me is what's caused me to crash and burn."

"I'd say that's a bit strong."

"What?"

"To say you've crashed and burned. It seems to me you pretty much have it all together."

She averted her gaze. "You're wrong. I'm far from having it all together. Just ask my boss."

When she heard the bitterness in her voice, Kelly tamped down the pain, then faced Grant again.

Sympathy filled his eyes, and for some reason, that made her angry. She didn't want his pity. She wanted his… Before that thought could mature, she slammed the door shut on it.

This was all too crazy; she had no idea what she wanted, especially from this man who had her mind and body going in all kinds of crazy directions. If she weren't careful—

"So that's why you're here?"

Kelly forced her mind back on track. She had started this in-depth inquiry into her life and she might as well finish it once and for all. "Yes. I wasn't working up to par, so my boss suggested I take a leave of absence."

"You didn't agree." Grant made it a flat statement of fact.

Kelly licked her bottom lip. She watched as his eyes concentrateD on the movement of her tongue. Refusing to acknowledge the feeling that shot through her, she said, "Not at first, but then I realized they were right. I really hadn't ever grieved for my family. I had just shoved the pain so far down inside me that it couldn't surface."

"Only one day it did. Unexpectedly."

"Exactly. I stayed at home for several weeks, during which I cried and pitched hissy fits. I also threw and broke things, but at least I was facing the pain. Then out of the blue, Ruth called, and here I am."

"Only not for long."

Her smile was empty, without humor. "The day Ruth returns, I'm leaving."

"This one-horse town's not for you, huh?"

"Those are your words, not mine."

"Still, that's the way you feel."

Kelly shrugged, hearing the slight censure in his voice. Too bad. Whether she liked it here or not wasn't any of his business. Yet in all fairness to him, she had vented to him. To turn around and insult him was not her usual *modus operandi*.

"Look, I didn't mean—"

Grant held up his hand, his mouth turned down. "Hey, you don't owe me an apology. At one time, I felt the same way."

Kelly's eyes widened.

"As you already know, I haven't always lived here."

"So you said, but you seemed to have found your perfect niche."

"In other words, it didn't take me long to turn into a country bumpkin."

Kelly felt herself flush. "I didn't mean—"

"Sure you did, and that's all right. I love these woods and all the people in them."

She didn't say anything else, knowing if she did, it would probably be the wrong thing. "What if you run out of trees to cut around here?"

"That won't happen."

"Really?"

He chuckled, then leaned forward.

Kelly got another whiff of his cologne, which once again assaulted her senses. She tried to pretend that it didn't bother her, but it was getting harder and harder by the minute. This man needed to go, especially since that hot kiss they had exchanged was very much on her mind. And if she even let herself think about how she'd felt when his finger grazed her breast, she'd be in big trouble.

"This area is a forester's haven," he said, jerking her back to reality. "I don't think I'll ever run out of trees."

"That's a plus for you."

"No matter, I love it here and hopefully won't ever have to leave it."

"I understand about that," Kelly said, vigor returning to her voice. "I love the city and never plan to leave it."

He cocked his head and gave her an assessing look. "I learned never to say never a long time ago."

"Does that include marriage?" Now why had she asked that? She was appalled at herself. She didn't care if he had been married, or if he'd ever get married, for that matter. Just because he'd kissed her with sound and fury didn't warrant digging into his personal life. "Sorry, that's none of my business."

"No problem." He shrugged with a grin. "I'm not

opposed to marriage, now that I've settled down in one place. I guess I just haven't run across the right filly with the right stuff."

A feeling of disgust suddenly swept through her. The right filly, huh? Such talk reminded her once again that she had absolutely nothing in common with this man and was wasting her time carrying on a personal conversation with him. He was going to be her client, nothing more.

As if he realized the climate in the room had changed, Grant stood slowly, that notable smirk appearing on his lips. "I've taken up enough of your time now."

Walking slightly behind him to the door, she couldn't help but notice his swagger which more than did justice to the tightest and best looking male behind she'd ever seen. Realizing the turn her thoughts had taken, Kelly sucked in her breath and muttered a dirty word.

"You say something?" he asked, turning at the door.

"No," she forced a smile.

His lips twitched, then grew serious, "You're still going to help me with the injunction, right?"

She thought a minute. "Are you sure you want me, since my firm certainly doesn't have much confidence in me at the moment?"

"You know better than that." Grant's tone as gruff.

She hesitated again.

"You can't jump ship on me now," he said.

"I told you I'd do what I could, and I intend to keep my word." She paused. "I just hope you won't be sorry."

"Oh, I won't be sorry," he murmured huskily, looking at her as if he could eat her up.

No, she told herself, don't let him mess with you like

this. Her feelings were purely physical. If she ignored them, they would go away.

"You know what I'd like to do about now, don't you?" The husky pitch has grown deeper.

That tightening in her chest increased, as if she were about to have a heart attack.

When she simply stood and stared at him, he added, "I'd like to kiss the hell out of you."

Then why don't you? she almost blurted out, and then sanity returned. Taking a steadying breath, she said, "I don't think that's a good idea."

"Me, either." He paused, raking hot eyes over her. "Because once I got started I couldn't stop with a kiss."

Kelly continued to stand unmoving, blood beating like a drum in her ears.

Putting his hat on, Grant tipped it, then cleared his throat, "I'll see myself out."

Once the door closed behind him, Kelly forced her legs to move to the sofa. She sank down and clutched her stomach, her mind and body reeling.

What had she gotten herself into?

Eight

"Got a minute?"

Grant scowled hearing the voice of his banker, Les Rains. "Got lots of 'em. Why?"

"Let's meet for coffee."

"Where?" Grant asked, hoping it wouldn't be at the Sip 'n Snack.

"Sip 'n Snack, Where else is there in this town."

Grant sighed inwardly. "See you shortly." He cut off his cell phone and headed in that direction.

As much as he'd like to see Kelly, he was reluctant to do so—even if it was all business. He enjoyed being around her far too much, and that bothered him. The last person he needed to see right now was the woman who pushed his buttons—in more ways than one. However, he'd best get used to it, since she was going to represent him. She *was* the only lawyer in town, like it or not.

All the more reason to keep his guard up. She had too much baggage to suit him. No way did he want to compete, *wouldn't* compete, with memories of a dead man and child. Entering a relationship where that was a factor would be suicidal on his part.

He figured no other man would ever live up to her husband. Hell, Grant didn't even want to try. When and if he married, and that was a big *if,* he'd envisioned his wife as a beautiful woman who would love the outdoors, same as he. She would work a garden alongside him, would even can fruits and vegetables. The thought of Kelly Baker doing any of those things brought a smirk to his lips.

Nope. She wasn't the woman for him. Yet he'd have to admit she was hot, and she made him hot. And tempted though he might be, it would serve him best to keep their relationship purely business. Not to mention that when their business was concluded and Ruth got back, Kelly would be heading out of Lane.

Grant had no intention of letting her take his heart with her, leaving a hole in his life as big as a crater.

No, sir. He was smarter than that.

A few minutes later, he walked into the Sip 'n Snack. Les Rains, was already seated with a cup of coffee in front of him. At first Grant didn't see Kelly, then she walked through the swinging doors behind the counter. When she spotted him, she pulled up short.

Their eyes met for what seemed an interminable length of time, then she nodded and headed in the direction of a table where a couple had just sat down. He figured she'd get to him next. But there was no hurry; the second he'd walked, her sweet perfume had surrounded him. He dared not look down, but he knew his manhood had probably risen to the occasion.

"You'll remember her the next time you see her."

Grant narrowed his eyes on his banker, whose face was as round as his body. Les wasn't fat; he was stout as a bull moose due to his daily workouts at a nearby gym. He said it kept him sane after dealing with crazies all day. Grant didn't envy him in the least dealing with people, especially about money. He'd much rather fool with equipment and trees. They were so much easier; they didn't sass back.

"What are you talking about?" Grant asked in a rough tone as he pulled out a chair and sat down.

Les snorted. "The way you were looking her over. What gives? You know her or something?"

"Sort of."

Les looked at Grant in sheer disbelief. "You can do better than that, my friend."

"What if I don't want to?"

Les grinned. "You looked like you could eat her with a spoon if you had one."

"Okay, so she's easy on the eyes. And I'm not dead, you know. So...?" Grant deliberately left his question open-ended.

Les's grin widened. "I was beginning to wonder. It's been such a long time since I've seen you with a woman or even heard you talk about one, for that matter."

"I'm too busy working."

"That's a crock."

Grant shrugged.

"Who is she, anyway?" Les asked. "And what's she doing here?"

"She's Ruth's cousin, Kelly."

"Ah, so it's Kelly, huh?"

Grant glared at his friend. "Go to hell."

"Hey, I don't blame you for giving her the once-over. Man, she's a knockout, not someone you'd ever figure would work in a place like this even if it is kind of classy for Lane."

"Ruth got in a bind and she's subbing for her."

"Whatever works."

Grant kept his mouth shut, preferring to watch Kelly as she took coffee and pastries to the table across from them. Today she had on a pair of black lowcut jeans, a wide belt, and black turtleneck sweater. Some kind of sparkly earrings dangled from her ears. Les was right; she was a knockout, especially today. Her outfit accentuated all the positives.

Before she saw him lusting after her, Grant averted his gaze. While the conversation between Les and him lagged, Kelly appeared at their table.

"Morning," she said in a slightly husky voice.

Grant looked up at her, and for a millisecond, their gazes locked again. "Morning to you."

"Coffee?"

"The strongest."

Kelly nodded. "I'll be right back."

Once she'd served them and left, Les chuckled. "Again, what's with you two? I saw the way *she* looked at you. Something's going on, but if you don't want to tell me, that's all right."

"Thank you," Grant said his voice loaded with sarcasm.

Les merely grinned.

"She's an attorney, actually."

Les's smile fled. "Her? An attorney?"

"That's what I said." Grant's tone was terse and low.

"Why is she here, then?"

"That's another story and frankly, it's none your business."

"Is that so?"

"Yes."

"I'm assuming you've made it yours, though."

Grant almost strangled on a smothered curse. "You just don't know when to give up or shut up, do you?"

"Nope."

"She's going to help me get the injunction lifted since Matt's out of the country. Are you satisfied now?"

"Way to go. I've never thought Matt was worth his salt, by the way."

Grant ignored Les's comment about his attorney. It didn't matter, anyway. Getting his men and equipment back on the job was all that counted. He sure hoped Kelly could do that. He was dying to ask if she'd started working on his case yet, knowing that she probably hadn't since they had just discussed it last evening. Still, he was impatient as hell.

Each wasted second cost him time and money.

Hopefully, she'd get started this evening. Therefore he had no intention of bothering her at home, though he wanted to. And that "want to" didn't have a thing to do with his case, either.

"So has she done anything for you yet?" Les asked.

"Not yet, I'm sure."

"She needs to get the lead out."

Grant frowned and was about to respond when Kelly showed up with a full pot of coffee. Once again, he felt his heart race just because she was near him. Damn. He'd better get a grip on his libido and his emotions.

"Need refills?" she asked, her gaze moving between them.

"No thanks," Les said. "Maybe later."

She nodded, then turned and walked off. Grant couldn't help but watch the sway of her cute derriere. He had to literally stifle a groan; he'd like nothing better than to grab that rear, swing her around and plant a kiss on those full, moist lips.

Forcing his mind off her took all the willpower he possessed, but he did it. The stakes were too high to dally.

"You're still in my corner on the money issue, aren't you?" Grant asked, his cup close to his mouth.

"I'll buy you as much time as I can," Les responded. "But the other powers that be aren't going to be as lenient." He paused. "If this mess takes a while to fix, that is."

"I understand," Grant said, feeling a churning in his gut he didn't like. "That's why I'm glad we talked. I need to keep Kelly posted on what's going on."

They talked shop a bit longer before Les finished his coffee and left. Grant walked up to the counter and perched on one of the stools. Kelly had her back to him, but then, as if she realized someone was looking at her, she whipped around. A veil fell over her face and eyes, making both totally unreadable.

"I just wanted to say bye and ask you to call when you know something."

She gave him a lame smile. "I will."

Their eyes held a moment longer, then he got up and walked out, his emotions suddenly so raw, so frightening, he cursed all the way to his truck.

Nine

After doing research on Ruth's computer, using the law library to search cases similar to Grant's, Kelly decided the county courthouse was her next stop. Wellington, the county seat, was just twenty miles away.

So the following day, once the coffee shop was closed to customers, she'd drove there and filed a motion to lift the injunction, in order to get Grant back in operation ASAP.

She wasn't sure what would happen. If Larry Ross was from around these parts, Judge Winston might extend the injunction rather than lift it—simply because in small towns, the good ol' boy network was almost always alive and well.

That wasn't fair, nor was it just, but she'd learned long ago that the United States legal system had huge holes in it. Still, it was the best and the most fair in the world, and she was proud to play a part in it.

Now, as she returned to Lane and was about to pull into Ruth's drive, she braked suddenly.

His truck was in front of the house.

For a second Kelly's sat immobile, her breath coming in quick sputs. Then she finally settled back to near normal.

Why did Grant have such an adverse affect on her? He made her think, and behave in a manner totally foreign to her.

But despite her attraction to him, Kelly remained firm in her conviction not to get involved with another man. The cost was too high. Friendship had been enough.

Until she'd met Grant.

Sure, he drove her crazy with his chauvinistic statements and devil-may-care swagger. But not only had he made her aware of her body, he had reawakened desires she'd thought were long dead and could never be resurrected. *Dead?* Ha! Was she ever wrong. The key, however, was not to give in to those desires, to be strong-willed and strong-minded. She had always considered herself both.

Now Kelly guessed, in the light of this new challenge, parked at her doorstep she'd see what kind of stuff she was made of.

With her limbs shaking far more than they should, she got out of the car. Grant met her halfway, his face looking as it had that day when he'd talked about Larry Ross—like a thunderhead ready to erupt. She squared her shoulders for bad news.

"Where the hell have you been?" he demanded in a harsh tone.

Taken aback at his sudden attack, Kelly's eyes widened. At the same time, perplexed anger shot through her. "Excuse me?"

"You heard me."

Her composure slipped. "How dare you talk to me that way?"

"How dare you just disappear."

"Hey," she retorted. "I don't have to account to you."

Grant muttered a foul word, than rubbed the back of his neck, as though buying time to regain control of his frustration and his temper. "Look, I didn't mean to go on the attack."

"Well, you did."

"Kelly—"

She ignored the pleading in his voice. "Get out of my way."

"Where are you going?"

"Inside the house, away from you." Kelly's eyes and tone were as frigid as she could make them. "No man talks to me like that and gets away with it. Certainly not one I barely know."

As if Grant realized he'd made a huge mistake with his confrontation, he gave her a contrite look. "Look, I'm sorry. Really sorry."

Kelly wrestled with her conscience. She would love to tell him to take a hike, actually to go to hell, but instead stated "I'm afraid 'sorry' won't cut it."

"I was worried, that's all."

She gave him an incredulous look, then wondered why she didn't simply skirt by him, go inside and put an end to this nonsense. Perhaps it was the desperate look in his eyes, or the fact that he was so darn attractive in his black Stetson, jeans, white shirt and boots. Not to mention his smell…as always, his cologne tickled her senses, making her slightly dizzy.

Damn him.

She took a steadying breath, then demanded, "Worried about what?"

"You."

"Me?" This time her tone was incredulous. "Why would you be worried about me?"

Where Grant's face was once heightened with color, it was now devoid of it. "I don't know. When you weren't at the shop or here, I thought maybe you'd—" He broke off and gave his neck a hard rub. "Hell, I don't know what I thought."

"I'm not leaving, Grant. I told you I would help you and I will."

She watched his entire body seemingly go into meltdown.

When he finally spoke, there was a desperate note in his voice. "But time is critical."

"I know that," she said, with as much patience as she could muster, especially when she still felt anger at his harsh display of emotion. Eddie had been such a gentle man, one who rarely got upset. Apparently it didn't take much to set this man's rockets on fire.

Because that thought actually excited her, her anger deepened. At herself.

"I spoke to my banker, and the bank's really nervous about the amount of money I owe," Grant added to the silence. "And when they found out about the injunction slapped against me, that added insult to injury."

"It's not as bad as it could've been," Kelly said. "While you were getting so bent out of shape, I was actually working on your behalf. I just got back from Wellington, where I filed a motion to lift the injunction."

Grant's features suddenly registered relief and remorse

before he said, "If you'd like to kick my rear, I'll be glad to bend over."

"Something tells me that wouldn't do any good."

She knew she'd scored a point because he flushed.

Then out of the blue, he asked, "Do you have anything to do right now?"

Kelly frowned "No, but—"

"Ride with me to the site, will you? Pete's out of town, and I need to check the equipment before it gets dark. On the way, you can fill me in on the details of your trip to Wellington."

Kelly's frown deepened. "I'm really not dressed for the woods." Actually, she was dressed in a pair of jeans, a camisole and jacket. It was just her delicate shoes that were all wrong.

"Hey, it doesn't matter. You don't have to get out of the truck unless you want to."

She threw up her hands in defeat. "I'd have better luck arguing with a stump than with you."

He grinned. "Stumps and I have a lot in common."

Kelly rolled her eyes. "Funny."

The second she crawled into the truck, which smelled like Grant, Kelly tensed. You'd think she would have learned not to get into intimate situations with him. Agreeing to help him was probably the most asinine thing she'd done in a long time.

Yet she'd so wanted to sink her teeth back into the practice of law. So far, she'd loved every minute of handling this easy case. Just walking into the courthouse earlier had given her a high like nothing else could. For a while she had meandered down the halls, inhaling that particular odor that only courthouses have.

No doubt about it, just serving coffee and grub was getting to her. But then, so was Grant. At the moment, the former was by far the safest to her peace of mind.

As if he picked up on her uneasiness, he faced her and said, "I promise to be on my best behavior."

"That's funny, too," she stated ironically.

"Hey, relax," he said as he turned on the engine and pulled away from the curb. "I know how you feel about the woods, but I promise you'll be safe."

Right now she wasn't worrying about the woods, but she couldn't tell him that.

"So did you talk to Judge Timmons?" he asked, drawing her attention back to him. She stared at his profile. Even that looked good.

"As a matter of fact I did, only he's not the judge hearing your case."

"That's a relief. I hear he can be a real pain."

"He was nice enough to me."

Grant shot her a glance. "You're a good-looking woman and he's a known ladies' man."

"Him? He must be in his eighties."

Grant laughed. "That old codger can apparently still romance according to the gossip mill, anyway."

She turned so he wouldn't see her smile.

"Sorry, didn't mean to embarrass you."

She cut her gaze back to him. "I'm not embarrassed. It's just the thought of him and a woman—" She broke off, now embarrassed at what she was about to say.

Grant tossed his head back and laughed. "I couldn't agree more."

A short silence followed his laughter, then he asked, "So

if Timmons isn't the one who issued the injunction, why did you spend time with him?"

"He and the founder of our firm go way back. Our paths just happened to have crossed and he asked me who I was—you know how a stranger sticks out—and we visited for a minute."

"So who's hearing my case?"

"Judge Winston, and I know zip about him, except that the injunction is temporary, which is definitely in your favor. Otherwise, this could drag on indefinitely."

Grant's features contorted. "That can't happen."

"Oh, but it can. However, that's what I'm trying to prevent. Hopefully, I can get a quick hearing date. At that time Winston will either enforce the injunction, limit it or strike it."

"When can you get this hearing?"

"We're on the docket for the end of next week."

Grant's features darkened. "Is that the best you could do?"

Clearly, Grant wasn't up on the typical schedules of the court. She flung him a chastising look. "Under the circumstances, you should be a little more grateful." There was an intentional sting to her voice.

Grant tugged at the corner of his lip. "You're right, I should say thank you very much for all your efforts on my behalf."

"A simple thanks will suffice."

Nothing else was said as Grant maneuvered his pickup onto a road leading to a cleared area filled with stacks of logs. Several pieces of huge equipment were parked there as well. She had never seen a logging site before. Curiosity getting the better of her, she commented. "Looks like most of the wood's already been cut."

"Hardly. We've barely started. What you're seeing is a log set. For each site, we clear a place where we stack the wood and store the equipment."

Grant got out of the vehicle. She did, too.

He looked at her through hooded eyes. "I thought you weren't getting out."

"I changed my mind."

"Suit yourself, but be careful."

She paused. "Are there snakes around?"

He gave her an indulgent smile, which unexpectedly made her heart turn over. "It's too cool for them to be out. Stump holes are your worst enemy. So watch your step."

"I'm sticking close to you."

Looking around, Grant said, "I don't see the skidder. I need to check on it."

Kelly peered about at the growing shadows among the thickets of trees still standing, and shivered. "Not without me, you aren't."

He laughed. "Come on, but again, take care."

Although she was careful not to touch him, she walked as closely as she could without doing so. "What are those markings on the trees?" she asked.

"Those are the ones to be cut."

She casts her eyes around. "Now I see. There seem to be tons left."

"Now you know why time is so critical. If we don't cut, no one makes any money. Not me, not the crew, not the bank."

"Ouch!" Kelly cried, feeling her right foot sink into a hole and turn.

Grant's hand shot out and caught her before she dropped

to her knees. Then he squatted to check her ankle. "You twist it?" he asked, his voice rough with concern.

Kelly put her weight on it, but kept her hand on his shoulder for support. "Don't think so," she responded in an unsteady voice. The incident frightened the frijoles out of her. What she didn't need was a broken or sprained ankle.

"I see the skidder," Grant said in that same rough tone. "Come on, let's get you back to the truck."

Twenty minutes later, Grant whipped the truck into Ruth's drive. During the ride, neither had said much. Kelly had wanted to ask him more questions about the job, but since he didn't seem to be in a talkative mood, she had kept her silence. Besides, her ankle felt tender, which made her furious at herself. If she'd remained in the vehicle, that episode wouldn't have happened.

Still, no real harm had been done, she assured herself. After a hot, soaking her body in hot water with Epsom salts she'd feel much better.

"Wait and I'll help you out," Grant said after he'd killed the engine.

"I'm okay. I can walk on my own."

He merely shrugged, but came around to open the door nonetheless. Good thing, too, because when she stood and put weight on her foot, she winced slightly. His hand shot out once again and grasped her arm.

"Thanks," she said, "but I'm sure it's okay. I guess I'm just a little paranoid."

"That's a good thing," Grant muttered.

Before she realized what was happening, he had swept her in his arms and carried her into the house. "I'm sure your ankle will be fine," he said roughly. "What about the rest of ya? Where?" he asked in a tight voice, stopping in the middle of the living room. "Sofa or bedroom."

She didn't dare look at him for fear of what he might read in her eyes. Every nerve in her body seemed on high alert, aware of being held so tightly in his arms.

When she kept her silence, he muttered, "How about here, on the sofa?"

His tone was low and husky, making it difficult to hear him. Her own throat was so constricted, she could only nod as he placed her on the cushions.

Then he seemed to freeze, He didn't withdraw his hands or move his face, which was as close as her next heartbeat.

Ten

Her breath caught. He was going to kiss her again, and she wasn't about to stop him. In fact, it was all she could do not to reach up and pull his head down to her lips, the ache inside her was so strong.

Then, to her astonishment and disappointment, Grant drew back. "Let me take a look at your ankle and foot," he said in a strangled voice.

Before she could react, he was on his knees in front of her, removing her casual shoe and trouser sock. She stilled herself not to react when he ran callused fingers over her foot and ankle, pressing gently around the slightly swollen area.

Though his eyes were smoldering when he finished, he let go of her foot. "It's going to be okay. Nothing's broken."

"So you think it's just bruised?"

"Yep," Grant responded. "Only slightly, it seems. But let's see how you do standing on it."

She complied and did just fine, though his hand supported her. "It's a bit tender, but otherwise okay. As long as it's not broken, I can deal with the situation."

Grant straightened. "Maybe I should help you to the bedroom, anyway."

She averted her gaze. "I'll be fine on my own."

"I'm not going to pounce on you, Kelly.'

"I know that." Her tone was sharp. She didn't know why that made her mad, but it did. Was she disappointed because he hadn't pounced?

Yes!

"Just wanted to clear the air in case there was some doubt."

"I think you'd best go." When she felt her chin begin to wobble, she turned away. Surely she wasn't going to become emotional because she really didn't want him to leave?

He cleared his throat. "You're right, I should."

"I hope you don't mind seeing your way out," she forced herself to say, still not looking at him.

She heard him move toward the door, but suddenly felt the sofa sink beside her. Her gaze whipped around at the same time a groan ripped through Grant. He reached for her, hauled her against him, and then, his eyes dark with desire, ground his hard, moist lips to hers.

It was just like she'd imagined. Lost in the moment's ecstasy, Kelly could only cling to him, returning kiss for kiss, knowing full well how quickly the situation could explode out of control, but not caring.

"I didn't mean for this to happen," he'd whispered

between hot, frantic kisses, leaning his heavy body half over hers so her breasts were pressed to his hard chest.

"Me, neither," she admitted breathlessly, continuing to cling to him as if she'd never let him go.

He looked deep into her eyes. "Want me to stop?" His voice sounded like rough sandpaper.

"Do you want to?"

"God, no."

"Then don't." How could she have said these words, especially to a man who wasn't her husband? Easy, she told herself. Her body had betrayed her.

Grant adhered his mouth to hers once again, pushing her back into the cushions. Then they both went a little wild, delving, probing and sucking with such hard, wet passion that Kelly felt as if the top of her head might come off. She knew if he dared touch her breasts or another intimate place, she would have an orgasm.

That was when he did just that.

With another groan, he pulled back, and without removing his gaze from hers, he pulled the straps of her camisole off her shoulders, then down her arms. Instantly, her breasts spilled in front of him. His eyes widened and he muttered, "So beautiful, so beautiful."

Kelly was powerless against the waves of feeling that pounded through her when his tongue bathed first one nipple, then the other. That was enough to do exactly what she'd feared—bring on a hard orgasm.

While the throbbing between her thighs went on and on, he buried his lips against her neck and whispered, "Oh, Kelly, I ache for you."

He reached for her hand and placed it on the protruding mound behind his zipper.

That movement was the catalyst that whipped her back to reality.

Without warning, she dragged her mouth off his, and with unsteady arms, pushed him away, placing some much-needed distance between them. But still she couldn't find breath enough to collect herself. She could only remain unmoving, continuing to feel the way his lips and tongue delved, probed, and sucked, leaving her mindless and aching.

"Kelly," he muttered roughly into the silence. "I—" His voice halted, as if he couldn't find the words to go on.

They stared at each other out of unreadable eyes, then he got up and stood in front of the fireplace.

"If you expect an apology, you can forget it," he said in a strained voice.

"I don't want an apology."

He blew out a breath. "Good."

"Although it wouldn't be wise to make a habit of this sort of thing."

A grin of sorts twisted his lips. "I rather enjoyed it myself."

She cut him a wry look. "That's my point."

He sobered. "I read you loud and clear, but I don't have to like it."

"Me, neither, but we both know—" She broke off abruptly.

He finished the sentence for her. "That this can't go anywhere."

"Right. We have no future together." Her voice was barely audible now. She was so shaken from how he had affected her, her insides still on fire. If he were to reach for her again, she would be a goner. She lowered her head to hide her thoughts.

"Kelly, look at me," he said in a gentle tone.

She didn't know why she complied but she did.

"I want you as much as you want me. Probably more," he stated. He paused, his eyes dipping south.

Automatically, hers followed suit, and her chest tightened. The bulge behind his zipper was there for the world to see.

"What can I say?" He shrugged with a lopsided smile. "He has a mind of his own."

Kelly felt color sting her face and she focused elsewhere. She shouldn't be embarrassed by what he'd said, but for some reason she was. After all, she'd been married for years. She hadn't been modest, or a prude, nor was she now. Maybe her discomfort was because the discussion was *so* personal between two people who barely knew each other.

Grant released a ragged breath, then said, "If I leave, are you sure you'll be okay?" He paused. "With your foot, I mean."

"It'll be fine," Kelly said with more conviction than she felt.

Still he hesitated. "Then I guess I'll go."

She heard the reluctance in his voice, but didn't acknowledge it.

Once Grant reached the door, he swung around and gave her another long look, then added, "Thanks for going with me."

"Thanks for taking me," she responded in a tight voice.

"Right," he muttered, then walked out, closing the front door behind him.

* * *

So how had it happened again?

Last night's intimacy was the first thing that crossed Kelly's mind when she woke the following morning. Even though she hadn't wanted to get any more involved with Grant, life didn't always go according to plan. Hadn't she learned that the hard way a long ago? In this case, however, no real harm was done.

Both she and Grant were grown-ups, of sound mind and body, with no ties, which made it perfectly okay if they shared a kiss or two.

Kelly winced. Only it had been more than that, she admitted, feeling a tremor along her nerves. They had engaged in a physical dance at its best. The kisses on both her breasts and lips had been hot, deep and personal, as if she and Grant had been trying to reach each other's souls.

Shuddering, Kelly glanced at the clock, then climbed out of bed, and headed for the bathroom. However, her progress was slow because of her foot, as well as thoughts of Grant.

Why did he have to taste so good? Always. And feel so good? She had never even thought about those things when it came to Eddie. What was the difference?

Feeling those erotic thoughts of Grant were somehow a betrayal of her late husband, Kelly lunged off the dressing stool, only to wince at the pain in her foot. She then made her way to the closet, donning a pair of paisley slacks, a camisole and jacket, as the February air remained quite chilly for Texas.

She peered into the mirror one more time, positive there would be tangible evidence that something different had happened to her—overly flushed cheeks, a glow in her eyes, something that would give away the fact that she and Grant had made love with their lips.

Nothing seemed changed.

Confident her secret was safe, Kelly went into the kitchen and made herself a cup of tea, hoping that would settle her nerves as well as revive her composure.

Then she phoned to set up an appointment with Larry Ross's attorney, Taylor Mangum. She hadn't told Grant her plans because they might not come to fruition. But if she was going to save him from bankruptcy, she had to move quickly.

As she finished her tea and peered into the empty cup, she wished she could do the same with Grant—empty her mind of him. She couldn't seem to do that. Brooding over her infatuation with him, however, wouldn't solve her problem.

The panacea for that was to keep busy.

Grabbing her purse, Kelly made her way out the door, dreading her next, unavoidable encounter with Grant.

He should've kept his hands—*and his mouth*—to himself, but he hadn't so there was no point in berating himself over something he couldn't change.

As soon as Ruth returned, Kelly Baker would be out of these woods as if her coattail was on fire. He couldn't blame her, either. He more than understood, because he felt the same way about the city. If the shoe had been on the other foot and he'd had to do a friend a favor—say in Houston—he'd be counting the days until he could haul his butt back to the country.

Then why did the thought of her leaving depress him?

He couldn't deal with the question, much less the answer. If he dwelled on that, it would send his thoughts back to the way she'd kissed him—like he'd tasted so good she could just eat him up.

When their lips had been burning each others and she'd sucked on his tongue, he'd wanted to rip off every stitch of her clothing, unzip his fly, lift her onto his lap and have her ride him until they were both exhausted.

If she hadn't pulled away when she did, Grant was afraid he might have totally lost control and done that very thing, which could have screwed up everything. She was his lawyer! Why couldn't he remember that.

His cell phone rang, thankfully putting an end to his torturous thoughts. It was Pete.

"Where are you?"

"Headed to Holland's," Grant said. "Thought I told you."

"You didn't, but that's okay."

"What's up?"

"Nothing. That's the problem. The crews are getting restless as hell, Grant. They're even talking about walking out."

Grant wasn't surprised, yet it upped his blood pressure and made him that much angrier at the situation. "That's why I'm headed to Holland's, to pressure him into talking to that so-called illegit brother."

"Good luck."

"Meanwhile," Grant added, "we still have Kelly working on the legal end. Tell the men to give it just a few more days. We'll get everything straightened out."

"Keep me posted."

Pete ended the conversation just as Grant reached the Holland ranch. As luck would have it, Dan was working on his driveway. He stopped and leaned on his shovel while Grant got out of his pickup and strode up to him.

"Nothing's changed," Dan said, an edge to his voice.

"I want to talk to Ross."

"I don't think that's a good idea. As a family, we've decided we're doing the right thing by settling this matter in court."

"That's all well and good for your family," Grant said with gushing sarcasm, "since you've got my money and invested it. While I, on the other hand, am left with nothing."

Dan's face lost its color. "I know it doesn't seem fair that we're sitting on easy street and you're struggling, but—"

"Cut the condescending crap, Holland, and get some balls. Get your brother out of the picture. You'll be doing the right thing by holding up your end of the deal. You took my money, I'm holding *you* accountable for this mess."

"I know, and I *feel* responsible."

"Then let's avoid a court hearing. Settle this between us."

"If only I could."

"Look, man, you're destroying my company. You've got me hung out to dry."

Holland's features remained stoic. "Trust me, I'm sorry about that, but I have no choice but to stick to my plan. My brothers feel the same way."

"If you ask me, you're all a bunch of fools for letting this so-called half brother hoodwink you."

Holland stiffened his back and glared at him.

Grant was tempted to deck him on the spot. Instead, he tightened his lips and glared back.

Then Dan muttered, "Oh, no," gazing past Grant's shoulder.

Grant swung around and watched as a man he'd never seen walked around the house toward them. Adrenaline shot through Grant's veins as he realized without asking who the man was.

This was turning out to be a good day, after all. "Well, well, if it isn't old Larry himself."

"Don't start anything, Wilcox," Dan warned.

"Or what?"

"You'll be sorry."

"I'm already sorry I ever did business with you."

Dan opened his mouth, only to slam it shut as Larry Ross stopped beside him. As if he sensed the tension in the air, he didn't say anything. He just bounced his eyes between Grant and Dan.

Ross was tall, but thin and pale, as though he needed some vitamins or a hefty helping of red meat. Or both. Grant figured if push came to shove, he could best the man with one hand tied behind his back. Hopefully it wouldn't come to that. But Grant wasn't making any promises to himself or anyone else. He'd do what was necessary to get his crews back cutting the timber he'd paid for.

"Grant Wilcox, Larry Ross," Dan said reluctantly.

Larry stiffened visibly. "I don't have anything to say to you."

"That's too bad, because I have plenty to say to you." Grant's voice was sharp and cold, though he didn't raise it.

"I don't have to listen to you, either."

"Says who?" Grant purposely egged him on for the sheer hell of it.

"My attorney."

"Look, why can't we be civil about this? Man to man. And keep the court out of it?"

"I'm happy working through the court."

Grant took a step forward. Ross backed up, fear written in the grooves in his face, as though he knew he was out-manned. "I suggest you settle this beef with your family really quick—like today. If not, I'll be back and I can promise you, you won't be happy to see me."

With that, Grant turned, jumped back in his truck and took off, his fingers gripping the steering wheel until his knuckles turned paper-white.

He knew his words meant nothing. Tearing that anemic-looking fellow from limb to limb wouldn't do anything but make Grant feel better.

Unless Kelly came through in the courts, he was dead in the water.

Eleven

"We're about to close, but if there's something I can get you, I'll be glad to."

"I came to see you, honey."

Kelly moaned silently. The last thing she needed was a last-minute customer, especially not one who came specifically to see her. Most people in this town didn't even know her, though she had to admit that was slowly changing. Discounting Grant, she had actually begun to make a few friends among her customers.

However, she didn't recall ever seeing this little old lady. If so, she would not have forgotten her. Talk about an unusual character; the tiny woman slowly making her way deeper into the shop was something else, especially for Lane.

She had to be in her late eighties if she was a day. Yet it was obvious she did everything in her power to disguise her age, from puttying up the cracks in her face with too much makeup, to wearing looped earrings that were almost bigger than her entire face.

No one could ignore her clothes either. She had on a pair of jeweled pants, a jeweled blouse, and jeweled jacket. She was so bright Kelly needed sunglasses to block the glare.

What a character.

"Through looking me over?" the woman asked without rancor.

Kelly was mortified and knew that it showed.

The woman waved a hand that sported long, thin fingers and heavily painted nails. "Don't worry about it, honey," she said with a chuckle. "Everyone's jaw drops when they first meet me—strangers, that is. Around here, everyone knows I'm crazy but harmless."

Kelly knew this offbeat woman might be harmless, but she sure didn't think she was crazy.

"By the way, I'm Maud Peavy." She reached out her hand and shook Kelly's. "Folks around here call me Ms. Maud. But I'll answer to near about anything."

Kelly laughed. "Well, Ms. Maud, I have to tell you up front you're my kind of lady. Kudos to you for still staying stylish at your age."

"Listen, honey, we never get too old to take care of ourselves. Remember that, will you?"

"My grandmother used to tell me the same thing."

"You fixin' to close, right?" Maud asked.

"That I am."

"Any plans?"

Kelly thought for a moment, then said, "No. Just go back to Ruth's, I guess."

"Come home with me instead."

Kelly blinked in astonishment.

Maud laughed. "Haven't you heard I'm famous for my homemade tea cakes?"

"Actually I haven't."

Maud frowned. "I'm kinda disappointed in my friends." As suddenly as the frown appeared, it vanished. "Surprises are good, too. So know that you're in for a real treat and don't even know it." She leaned her head that had very little hair left on it.

What surprised Kelly was that she didn't wear a wig to offset that flaw since she was so style conscious.

As if she read Kelly's mind, Maud patted the top of her head. "Doctor told me I couldn't wear my wig for a while. I've had some kind of crud in my scalp." She shook her head. "You know how these doctors are. If you don't do what they say, then they won't see you anymore."

Kelly hid a smile, never having had that experience, but then she wasn't from a postage-stamp-size town where the people acted and did things differently than in the city.

"So are you coming?" Maud asked, noisily clearing a frog from her throat.

"Of course. But would you mind if I went to Ruth's first and got comfortable? I also have a phone call to make."

"Take your time, honey. That'll give me the opportunity to whip up a fresh batch of tea cakes and put them in the oven."

"Mmm, that sounds heavenly."

"Honey, when you taste one, you'll think you died and entered those pearly gates."

Kelly laughed outright, and it felt so good, so liberating, it gave her cause for serious thought. Maybe her doctor had been on target when he'd forced her to take a leave of absence from the firm. Rarely had any spontaneous laughter erupted there.

Maud gave her directions to her house, then said, "I'll see you shortly," before making her way back to the door.

A short time later Kelly had changed her shoes and clothes. For her own secret pleasure, she removed both bra and panties, since her warm-up suit was thick and showed no signs of her nudity underneath.

Already feisty Maud had been good for her, giving her the courage to be herself and to do something a bit outrageous, if you will, without worrying about what someone else would think.

Fifteen minutes later, she walked in Maud's modest home. The old lady had yelled from the kitchen telling her the door was open.

The wonderful aroma of freshly baked cake stopped Kelly in her tracks, and she inhaled deeply. She hadn't smelled anything this good since her grandmother had died. Although Grammy never made tea cakes, she did have a specialty of her own—a pound cake made with coconut, extra eggs and butter. It never failed to melt in Kelly's mouth. She suspected that would be the case with Maud's tea cakes.

"The flavor of the day will be plain ones," the eccentric woman announced as Kelly strolled into the small, cluttered kitchen. "I want you to taste the real thing first. Later, I'll put icing some."

Kelly smiled. "Beggars can't be choosers."

"Pooh, you're no beggar, just malnourished. You're skin

and bones!" Maud nodded toward the table. "Just dump that stuff out of the chair onto the floor and have a seat."

Kelly smiled and did as she was told, placing the pile on top of the things already in the opposite chair.

Maud turned and faced her, leaning against the kitchen cabinet near the sink. She had on an apron, and a bandanna tied around her head. A smudge of flour almost covered one rouged cheek. Her new friend was definitely a sight, Kelly thought. But she wouldn't have missed this adventure for anything.

None of her cohorts at the firm would believe her if she told them about this eccentric woman, so she wouldn't even bother. Even if they did believe her, her lawyer friends might look down their noses at Maude. Suddenly Kelly squirmed in her seat. At one time, she probably would have, too.

"So whatcha want to drink?" Maud asked. "Tea, coffee, milk, half-and-half?"

"Half-and-half?" Kelly's eyes widened on Maud. "You mean people actually drink that with your cookies?"

"Of course, honey. But let's get something straight. What you're about to honor your mouth with are not cookies. They are authentic tea cakes. No one besides me has the recipe."

"Will you ever share your recipe?"

Maud thought about that. "Don't know yet. Haven't decided who's worthy of it, although Ruth has begged me to let her bake and sell them."

Kelly chuckled. "Only you won't."

"Hell no, then people wouldn't come to my house. They'd go to Sip 'n Snack." Maud came a little closer, then lowered her voice as though someone else might hear. "She's sorta my competition."

Kelly giggled. "Ah, so I get it now. You like the company."

"I love company. Fills my otherwise lonely days to the brim."

"Seems like you're one of a kind, Maud Peavy."

Maud smiled, then peered so hard at Kelly she almost squirmed in her seat. "Most people think you're kind of stuck on yourself, you know."

Oh, great.

"I'm sorry they feel that way," Kelly responded, for lack of anything better to say. That out-of-the-blue statement set her back a bit, yet she wasn't surprised at the assessment. But in defense of herself, she felt as if she'd been tossed onto another planet and expected to fit right in. Well, life didn't happen that way.

"Only they're wrong. You're nice," Maud said, breaking Kelly's train of thought. "In fact, you're real nice. And pretty as a picture, too."

"Thanks," Kelly said, feeling a flush steal into her cheeks, though she was unable to figure out why. There was just something about this town, these people that baffled her, yet intrigued her, too. Especially this kind and eccentric soul.

"I know Grant thinks you're pretty, too."

Kelly went still. "You know Grant?" Silly question, she told herself. Everyone knew everyone in this town, even their personal business.

Maud chuckled. "When he leaves the woods most days, this is the first place he hits. He can scarf down a dozen of my cakes in one sitting."

"I don't doubt that."

Maud paused and narrowed her eyes. "I understand you're trying to help him get back to work, you being a lawyer and all from one of those fancy firms."

"I don't know about my firm being fancy, but I am trying to help him."

"I'm glad. He's my most favorite person in the world."

That statement shocked Kelly. Rough Grant and bejeweled Maud were *friends?* "Is he related to you?"

"No. I love him like he was, though. All my family's dead. Even when they were alive, most of 'em weren't fit to know or kill."

Kelly laughed. "Most people would never admit that."

"I understand you lost your family," Maud said, her face and tone now sober. At one time Kelly would've been offended that her business had been bandied about town. Now it didn't seem to matter. Had she changed that much since coming to Lane?

Perhaps.

"I lost a great husband and precious daughter."

"I'm so sorry. You deserve better."

"Thank you. But life can kick you in the teeth," Kelly whispered, purposely biting into another tea cake. "Oh, my gosh, this is heavenly."

Maud grinned as she poured Kelly a cup of half-and-half. "You never said what you wanted to drink, so I made the choice." She winked. "You won't regret it."

Kelly laughed and merely shook her head.

"So, how do you and Grant get along?" Maud asked in a crisp voice, changing the subject.

Kelly was taken aback, giving Maud carte blanche to keep on going. "I think he kind of likes you."

Though flustered and frustrated at the turn in the conversation, Kelly didn't alter her benign facade. Curiosity, however, got the better of her and prompted her to ask, "Did he tell you that?"

"Didn't have to. I know him better than he knows himself."

Cool it, Kelly, she warned herself, feeling color return to her face. This old woman was smarter than a fox in a hen house. And if she was on a fishing expedition for herself, or whomever else, Kelly wasn't about to bite the hook.

"So how do you feel about him?" Maud asked bluntly, placing a plate of hot tea cakes in front of her. For a moment Kelly couldn't respond; she was too eager to snatch a cake and eat it.

"Go ahead, dig in." Maud chuckled. "We can talk about Grant after you've had your fill of my delicacies."

Even as she reached for another cake, Kelly almost blurted out that Grant was off-limits. But she knew she'd be wasting her time and her words. This woman marched to her own drummer and would say exactly what she pleased, when she pleased.

"Can you help him?" Maud asked after they had both consumed their fair share of the cakes.

"I certainly hope so."

Maud looked pensive. "That boy's worked so hard to get where he is, sacrificed so much, that I'd hate to see it all go down the drain now."

"That's what I'm hoping to prevent."

The old woman nodded. "Good girl."

This time Kelly chose to change the subject, but not before drinking the last of her milk. "I don't think I've ever tasted anything as good as these cakes."

"See, I told you so."

"No wonder Ruth is itching to sell your goodies."

"Not going to happen," Maud said again, "though I'm flattered. Besides, Ruth's doing great with her thing. Right?"

"As far as I can tell, she is." Kelly shrugged. "But then you know I'm like a fish out of water. Selling coffee and soup isn't my forte."

"Then why are you here?"

"I came to help Ruth out."

Apparently Grant hadn't said anything more about her problems, just about Eddie and Amber. Kelly's estimation of him shot up a notch, but that didn't mean anything special, she assured herself hurriedly. He was just someone she'd met in this town whom she'd agreed to help. Nothing more, nothing less.

Even though she'd just met Maud, she felt like she could open up to her as a friend. "I almost had a nervous break-down," Kelly admitted.

Maud reached out and covered her hand. "You did right by coming here, young lady. This country air and us country folk will help you heal."

Sudden tears rose in Kelly's eyes. She blinked them back. "I never thought of it like that, but maybe you're right. A change of venue just might do the trick."

"Sometime I'd like to see a picture of your family."

Kelly reached into her purse for a tissue. "Sometime I'll show you one."

Maud smiled. "I like you, Kelly Baker. I like you just fine."

"And I like you."

"You come see me anytime you want," Maud said

staunchly. "You'll always be welcome. And if you can't sleep, I'm at my best at three in the morning."

Kelly laughed and reached for another tea cake even though her stomach felt as if it was going to pop. But she didn't care. She didn't know when she'd get another opportunity to visit Maud. She expected Ruth to return sooner than later.

And she couldn't forget about Grant's case. She had her work cut out for her on it.

"I've got a batch ready for you to take home," Maud said, interrupting her thoughts.

"What about me?"

Kelly froze.

Not so Maud. Upon hearing Grant's voice she whirled around, walked over and gave him a big hug. Kelly, looking on, hoping her mouth wasn't gaping, watched as the old woman almost disappeared into his big body.

"I've told you about sneaking in," Maud scolded, punching him in the chest. "That's not nice."

"I always just walk in."

Maud sniffed. "It's different today. I'm entertaining a very distinguished guest."

Feeling embarrassed, Kelly rose and said, "Come on, Maud, give me a break."

"Sit back down, young lady," she ordered. "You're not going anywhere."

"Yes, she is," Grant said with ease.

"Oh, no, she isn't."

Kelly stared at one then the other, undecided who she wanted to strangle first. "Actually, I'm going home."

"I'm cooking steaks," Grant said, his gaze locked on her, freezing her in place. "I thought you might come over and we'd discuss the case."

"Good idea," Maud said in a cheery voice, facing Kelly. "You could use some meat on those bones."

Although Kelly steamed inside, she wouldn't hurt Maud's feelings for anything. Grant, however, was a different matter. "What I have to say can be said over the phone."

"So you do know something?" Grant asked in an eager tone.

"I spoke with Larry Ross's attorney."

"Sounds like you two have a lot to talk about." Maud walked over to Kelly and kissed her on the cheek. "Go on with him, honey. It'll be all right. He'll have to answer to me if he doesn't treat you right."

"Maud, you're meddling again," Grant said in a kind but stern voice.

Kelly felt trapped. For some crazy reason that she didn't even understand, she wanted to go with Grant. The thought of spending another evening alone didn't bear thinking about. Yet the thought of spending it with *him* didn't bear thinking about, either.

"I can't stay long," she said in a rather stilted voice.

Grant shrugged. "It's your call."

"Wonderful," Maud said with a Cheshire cat smile. "You two run along now and tend to business. I'll talk to you both later."

Kelly looked at Grant, who winked, then motioned for her to go ahead of him. She could always leave, she reminded herself, if things didn't go her way. Maybe that was the problem. When it came to Grant, things rarely went her way.

With insides quivering, she walked with him out the door into the twilight, feeling his eyes track her every step.

Twelve

"So how was your steak?"

Kelly smiled, then stretched until she felt Grant's eyes, with fire in them, peruse her body. Although they hadn't had anything to drink, she suddenly felt dizzy, as if she'd consumed a glass of strong wine.

That kind of feeling was exactly why she shouldn't have accepted his invitation to dinner. But what choice had she had? Maud and Grant had ganged up on her. If she'd made a stink about not joining him, Maud would have certainly read more into Kelly's refusal than was there.

A no-win situation!

She had wanted to have dinner with Grant. The second he'd walked through Maud's door, every nerve in Kelly's body had awakened. They were still in that state, though he'd made no effort whatsoever to touch her. Throughout the preparation of dinner—from grilling the steaks and corn, to making the salad—he'd been the perfect gentleman and host.

Yet every time they came within touching distance, she reacted inside. Her nerves tightened that much more. She sensed his reaction was the same as she'd caught him throwing her several smoldering looks when he didn't think she was watching.

Now that dinner was over and, at her insistence, the kitchen tidied, they were now seated in his rustic living room. A fire was burning and a romantic Alan Jackson CD was playing on the stereo system.

A perfect place and a perfect night for making love.

Horrified, she reined in her raw thoughts. If she didn't hurry and get back to Houston, she was going to be in big trouble.

"You're not talking?"

Kelly cut her eyes toward him and saw the humor lurking around his mouth and eyes. She heard it in his voice, too. "And you think all lawyers talk too much, right?"

"Yep. Except the one sitting on the sofa beside me."

Kelly smiled. "I guess my mind was wandering. But to answer your question, the steak was delicious as was everything else."

"Good." His gaze rested on her for a heartbeat. "I wanted you to enjoy."

"Well, you accomplished your goal."

Small talk. That was all they were doing, trying to ignore the sexual tension closing in around them.

"We need to talk," she finally said.

"Yeah, we do," Grant replied with a sigh as though disappointed that the erotic spell was broken.

"I spoke to Ross's lawyer, Taylor Mangum, today."

Grant sat a little straighter. "And?"

"I told him that I was calling out of courtesy to ask him to convince his client to take a voluntary DNA test."

Grant slapped his palms together. "Way to go. That would knock this issue in the head one way or the other."

"I went on to tell Mangum," Kelly added, "that if Ross refused, I would file a motion with the court to force him to take the test, proving whether he is or is not an heir."

"Go on." Grant's tone held rigid excitement.

"Mangum said he'd talk to his client, but doubted he'd comply."

Grant's features darkened. "Why wouldn't Mangum insist that he take it?"

"No sweat off his back whether he does or doesn't," Kelly acknowledged. "The longer this strings out, the more money Mangum makes."

Grant cursed. "Is that what all lawyers are about—making money?" Then, as if he realized what he'd said and to whom, he muttered another curse, then said, "Sorry, didn't mean that."

"Yes, you did, but that's okay. You're right. Money is what some lawyers are all about. Me, too, but I also care about doing what's right for my clients and for justice."

Grant smiled at her. "That firm's damn lucky to have you. I hope they know that."

She merely nodded, feeling tears press against the back of her eyelids. One minute this man was a rough forester with no class, and the next a smooth-talking man with tons of class. Perhaps that was what attracted her: he was an enigma.

"If Ross is legit like he claims, then why would he resist?"

"Taking a DNA test for whatever reason is frightening to most people, thanks to the horror stories in the media about how DNA and other tests are horribly misused and abused."

"So if he refuses, which Mangum suspects he will, how long will it take to get the matter heard in court?"

"Depends on how soon we can get on the docket."

"Damn," Grant muttered. "This whole legal thing moves far too slow to suit me. The bank could call in my note before I ever get inside a courtroom."

"Maybe not. Remember the injunction hearing is next week." Kelly injected a light note in her voice. "Who knows, maybe Ross will jump at the chance to take a DNA test."

"I doubt that, if for no other reason than to spite me and take delight in shutting me down permanently."

"Have you talked to him?"

"Yep."

"That wasn't smart."

Grant rubbed his jaw. "It's just one of those quirky turns of fate." Then he told her how he'd run into Larry Ross at Dan Holland's house.

"As long as you didn't take a swing at him, I think we're okay."

"You have no idea how much I wanted to deck him."

"Oh, I think I do." Kelly felt her lips twitch.

Grant gave her a sheepish grin before his features sobered once again.

"Like I said, try not to beat up on yourself," Kelly said,

her tone encouraging. "We might get lucky and Winston might force Ross to take the test."

"You think?"

"That's a possibility. Most judges don't like people who waste their time, and if one simple swab in the mouth will settle a case, then he or she usually won't hesitate to order it."

"Again, it's just getting to that courtroom." Grant's tone was harsh with disgust. "Meanwhile, I'm hanging out to dry."

"Surely your friend at the bank won't let them foreclose."

"We'll see." Grant then filled her in on his conversation with Les.

Afterward, they sat in silence for a few minutes, each of them gazing at the fire as though mesmerized by the glowing flames.

Grant finally reached over, took her hand and pulled her up. She lifted astonished eyes to him, her thoughts distracted from the case.

"Let's dance," he whispered, drawing her against his chest.

Alabama was singing, "If I Had You," a song that Kelly had heard on a C & W channel several times and liked very much. In fact, she'd considered buying the CD, only she hadn't taken the time.

"I guess I should ask if your ankle's up to boot scootin'?"

"My ankle's not a problem."

Grant began to move, and she with him, step for step.

"Mmm," he said, two-stepping her around the wooden floor. "For a city girl, you know how to move."

"Country and western dancing's really not my thing," Kelly said in a breathy voice, her head reeling for more reasons than one. She loved being held in his arms, his body grazing hers, especially when he twirled her.

Careful, Kelly, she warned herself silently, feeling her past rise up and intrude on this moment, threatening to plunge her into bitter sorrow. No matter; she didn't want him to let her go. Her breathing was becoming ragged and fast.

"You couldn't prove it by me," he said, his own voice sounding foreign, as if his throat was scratchy. "You're smooth as glass."

"You're just trying to make me feel good," she whispered.

"Oh, honey," he said, peering down at her, "that's a given. You feel so damn good I don't want to let you go."

That should've been the signal that it was time to call a halt to this craziness and go to Ruth's. Instead, Kelly continued to dance with him through several more songs. It was the last one, "There's No Way," that was the culprit that slowed them to a crawl. Before she knew it, they were belly to belly, hip to hip, then he was grinding his lips to hers.

Still, their bodies moved in time to the music while he explored her lips with his mouth.

Finally Grant withdrew, and while not dancing per se, they swayed as one.

"I should go," Kelly said in a barely audible voice.

"Why?"

"Because."

"Because why?" Grant's own voice was raspy.

Because I'm frightened of what you're doing to me, how you make me feel, as if I'm losing myself. "I—" she began, only to be interrupted.

"Stay with me. Please. You want me and I want you."

"I do. I do."

And she did. And she felt no shame for that, either. It

had been so long since she'd felt a man's mouth, tongue and hands on her body. She knew without a doubt that Grant would be that kind of lover. It would be all or nothing with him.

Was that wrong? Was *she* wrong? No, not if she could keep her heart out of the equation and enjoy making love for what it was—a release for her mind and body.

Could she do that? Maybe not. At this point she didn't know, nor did she care. Tomorrow she might be consumed with remorse and regret. But not tonight, not when she ached so desperately for him.

As if to settle the argument going on inside her head, Grant boldly placed her hand on his swollen manhood. Then he placed his hand on her swollen breast.

When Kelly didn't remove either, he added, "That's about as good as you can get between two people."

And it was.

She wanted him to quench that fiery hunger raging inside her so badly she couldn't even speak.

"You're so lovely," Grant whispered, as he stopped and slowly unzipped her warm-up jacket. When he saw she was braless, he drew in a breath and his eyes widened. "Again, so beautiful. So perfect."

He touched her breasts, first one then the other. Kelly felt her knees buckle under the tender assault, especially when he lowered his lips and sucked and kept on sucking.

After that, they'd shed their clothes posthaste, then knelt together on the thick rug in front of the fire, lips locked in a kiss as hot as the flames licking their naked bodies.

Then Grant laid her down and began licking her flesh, starting with her breasts and working his way downward.

When he reached the apex of her thighs, he paused and looked at her, a question in his eyes.

Caught up in the heat of the moment and the need to have him any way she could get him, Kelly didn't utter a word. Taking her silence as consent, he lowered his head and used his tongue until orgasm after orgasm pelted her.

No! she cried silently. She didn't want to feel this emotional intimacy with this man. This was a matter of the heart. Even if she wanted to, she couldn't give hers. It had been taken long ago by her husband, and she couldn't betray that love.

Yet she couldn't stop Grant's tongue, nor did she want to.

After moaning and thrashing, she whispered, "Please," digging her fingers in his flesh and urging him up and over her.

"Oh, baby, baby," he groaned, thrusting his hardness into her wet softness. Then he pounded flesh against flesh until they both cried out.

When they were drained, he rolled her over on top of him. They lay like that until their heartbeats calmed.

She had felt him in every part of her—even her heart.

She felt as though his heart and mind were inside her as well-merged with her soul. This was more than sex. That was exactly what she wanted to avoid. When she went back to Houston, she intended to leave fully intact, heart included. Leaving it behind was *not* an option.

Following a satisfied sigh, Grant eased her off him. Then he turned her so they were face-to-face. "That was incredible. *You're* incredible."

"So are you," Kelly managed to say around the lump in her throat, pulling back and looking at his body from head to toe, taking in the hard muscled chest, his hair in all the right places, his steely legs.

"You're perfect," she declared.

"You're unbelievable. I want you again. Now."

"Now?"

He nodded.

Without hesitation, she straddled him, then paused and stared down into his dazed eyes. "You like?"

"I could get addicted to this, to you," he said in a voice that sounded as if he was hurting.

Hadn't she already risked enough of her heart for this man? Kelly's answer, however, was to move slowly, then fast, then faster, riding him until they both froze in ecstasy.

Then with one last cry, she fell on top of him, their hearts beating as one.

Thirteen

Kelly was the first to awaken. For a moment she was completely disoriented, but then it hit her: she was at Grant's house. She was on the floor—in front of a fire that was barely alive. Had she been there all night? Yes. The incredible magenta-colored sunrise peeping through the window bore testimony to that. For a moment the beauty of it took her breath away. It was one of the loveliest sights she had ever seen.

She'd never glimpse that in the city, she told herself.

Then she peered at Grant who was either still asleep or pretending to be. Either way, he wasn't stirring, but he needed to be. And so did she. The coffee shop had to be opened. While Doris and Albert could certainly unlock the doors, they were unwilling to work at the front unless an emergency occurred.

And this was no emergency.

Yet Kelly didn't move. She felt too warm and comfortable. *Too loved*. Panic knotted her stomach, then she relaxed. Making love was not the same as *being* in love, she reminded herself. Hence, she didn't intend to agonize over last night.

She had enjoyed every second of their hot and passionate lovemaking. It had been an incredible experience. Grant was a perfect lover. Even better than Eddie, she admitted with only a prick of conscience.

And she had unashamedly loved Grant back. As she'd realized, they were grown-ups and didn't have to justify their actions to anyone. Neither was married and neither had a significant other.

So why weren't they a match made in heaven?

"My, but you look like you have the weight of the world on your shoulders."

Kelly had been so lost in thought she hadn't been aware Grant had awakened and was watching her. "I'm okay," she said with a tentative smile, wondering about his take on last night.

Instead of answering her silent question right off, he merely drew her closer to his naked body, making sure the afghan was securely wrapped around them, warding off the chill.

"I loved every second of being inside you," he finally whispered in her ear, as he outlined it with the tip of his tongue.

Shivers darted through her. "I loved it, too."

He placed a hand between her legs which sent several more shivers through her. "You have the most gorgeous body."

"When I can find time, I work out at a gym near the

firm." Kelly could barely talk; her throat was simply too tight, especially as his hand was gently moving up and down her inner thigh, pausing in all the right places.

"I can tell."

"Tell what?" she asked inanely.

Grant chuckled, obviously aware he had rattled her and that she wasn't making much sense.

"No regrets?"

Kelly took a deep breath, knowing without asking what he was referring to. "No regrets."

"Me, either."

A short silence followed.

"I didn't hurt you, did I?"

Her heart fluttered. "No, not really."

"You gotta be a little sore."

In spite of herself, Kelly felt color creep into her cheeks, which, under the circumstances, was ridiculous. She was glad he couldn't see her face.

Grant pulled her even closer, leaving no doubt that he was as full and hard as she was wet. "You haven't been with anyone since your husband died?"

"No." Her throat constricted.

"I still can't comprehend how it would be to have a family one day and the next no one." He paused and clasped one of her hands in his. "You're a strong woman, Kelly Baker."

His voice had grown so thick and husky Kelly could barely hear him.

"And I admire the hell out of you," he added.

"Please don't say that. If you only knew." Her voice broke. Sensing how distressing this subject was to her, Grant pulled her tight against him, positioning himself between her thighs. She gulped silently and didn't move.

He tongued her ear again. "I could get used to this."

"To…to what?"

"Waking up with you in my arms. But I'd prefer a bed."

She heard the smile in his voice and it warmed her heart. Too bad there were so many differences between them. He was a wonderful lover, only she wasn't looking for a lover. She wasn't looking for a man, period….

Her purpose in Lane was to heal her mind and her body, then to return to the work she loved—in the city.

"What are you thinking about?" Grant asked in a whisper.

"How close I came to losing my mind."

"Like I told you before, I don't know how you even functioned." He paused. "You're way too hard on yourself."

"There's something you don't know about me."

"It doesn't matter."

"It does to me."

"So you want to tell me?"

She nodded. "I sort of lied to you."

"I'm listening."

"The time I took off work, I actually spent in a special care facility." She couldn't bring herself to say the word *institution*. Her stomach roiled at the thought.

"And you see that as something to be ashamed of?"

"Yes, I guess I do."

"Well, I say bully for you for admitting you needed help and getting it."

"I really had no choice. When the firm sent me home that first time, I fell apart. Although I was going to a counselor, that wasn't cutting it. I went on crying jags, pitched hissy fits, threw things. That's when I realized I was totally out of control, and checked myself into the facility."

"Oh, baby, I'm so sorry," Grant whispered his mouth against her neck.

She shivered.

"Shh, it's okay. You're going to be just fine. In fact, you're going to be more than fine. You've got what it takes—trust me on that. You'll end up putting that firm on the map."

Kelly turned in his arms and faced him, knowing tears were cascading down her cheeks. With a groan, he carefully and slowly licked the tears as they fell from her eyes.

"You're a remarkable woman. Don't ever forget that." He tapped her on the nose. "I bet one day God will give you another child."

"No he won't, because I don't intend to marry again."

"Never say never."

She ignored that and asked, "What about you?"

"What about me?"

"Don't you ever long for a permanent home?"

"I got one." His voice was lower than husky. "If I'm not mistaken, you're in it right now."

She scrutinized him noticing his bittersweet smile. "You know what I mean."

"Sure do," he drawled. "A home in suburbia with a wife, and two point three children and a dog."

"If that's the way you want to define it, yes, that's what I mean." She paused intentionally, then said, "I assume you never long for that."

"I can't say I haven't thought about it. But long for, no, I guess I haven't."

"Which means you haven't ever been wild about a woman."

"I had one serious relationship," Grant said painfully.

"What happened?" Kelly pressed, giving in to her need to pry.

"It didn't work out."

She waited for him to elaborate.

Grant sighed, as though he knew he had no choice but to say more. "She wanted me to join her dad's company in Dallas."

"Bottom line, she didn't want to live in rural America?"

"You got it."

Kelly listened for any bitterness in his tone, but found none. "What about the others?"

"We either drifted apart or became just good friends."

"Looks like you've never felt the need to make a commitment to marriage."

"Guess not. At least not enough to make it happen."

They were silent for a long moment.

"However, under different circumstances, you, Kelly Baker, could change my mind."

Though Kelly was taken aback, she rebounded. "But the circumstances are what they are and we can't change them."

"Right." Grant muzzled his lips against hers. "But this isn't a fantasy—your body next to mine—which means I'm going to act out a portion of my fantasy right now."

Wiping out all thought of a future that was never to be, Kelly sighed, slipped her leg over his thigh, sighed again as he entered her.

Simultaneously, their cries rent the air.

* * *

"Top of the morning to you, Ms. Baker."

"Good morning, Mr. Mangum."

"My, but aren't we formal," Kelly said with a tinge of sarcasm, and then felt bad about her lack of professionalism.

"I guess that's because what I have to tell you is formal." Mangum paused and cleared his throat. "More or less."

"Your client refuses to take a DNA test." She didn't ask a question.

"That's right and I think that's a wise decision."

"We'll see if the judge agrees with you."

"Good luck, young lady."

Kelly didn't bother to answer the condescending jerk. She simply hung up, and this time her lack of professionalism felt damn good.

Mangum's call had caught her between the breakfast and lunch rush, although she couldn't say she'd been all that *rushed*. Business was off a tad, and she hoped that had nothing to do with her. The townsfolk loved Ruth and missed her smile and her ability to chat with them. They obviously had no qualms about telling Ruth anything and everything about their lives.

With Kelly it was different. She didn't know the customers, though she'd tried to learn the regulars' names and felt she'd done an adequate job of that. Still, she had a long way to go before she became the people person Ruth was. But then, she had never wanted to be.

Hopefully she would soon be packing her car and heading back to Houston. *Without Grant.* Suddenly a sick feeling invaded her stomach. She got up from the chair in

Ruth's tiny office and walked to the window and peered out at the sunshine.

A perfect day for Grant to be in the woods. She knew he was going stir-crazy because he wasn't there. Right now, she had done all she could. The next move was the court's.

She wondered what he was doing at this particular moment. Was he thinking about her?

Kelly drew a trembling breath. Since she'd left his house, she'd thought of little else. Their coming together had been incredible, and even now, as much as he'd loved her body from end to end and everywhere in between, she craved more.

Had Grant turned her into a sex fiend? She laughed at the thought.

After Eddie's death and before she'd met Grant, she hadn't cared if a man ever touched her again, much less made love to her. Now, after a long lapse, she was addicted.

Too bad. She'd just have to get over her addiction, go through detox of a different kind, because she was going back to Houston *alone*.

She had survived the worst possible trauma that could happen to anyone. As Grant had pointed out, she was still functioning, albeit not as well as she could be. But she was getting there.

Returning to Houston and to her firm was what she wanted most. A thrill of anticipation shot through her. Starting to handle Grant's case had reminded her that she loved being a lawyer—and couldn't wait to return to work.

If only she didn't feel a pinch of sadness at the thought of leaving Lane. She didn't want to feel anything for this small town or any of the people who lived in it. Unfortunately, she did. She really liked Ms. Maud. Since she'd visited the old lady, Kelly could see them becoming close. And those tea cakes. They were to die for. She couldn't imagine not ever eating another one.

Besides Maud, there were other customers she'd come to know and like.

Then there was Grant. She couldn't imagine leaving him. But she knew when the time came, she could and *would* do it.

And never look back.

Fourteen

"It won't be long now."

"So you're about to wrap things up in Montana and head back to the woods of East Texas, huh?"

Ruth laughed. "That's right, so try and contain yourself. I know you're jumping through hoops to get back to Big H."

Not necessarily, Kelly was tempted to say, but didn't for fear of the questions that would follow. No doubt Ruth would be shocked.

"It's been an experience, I'll admit," Kelly said.

"Lordy, I can't wait to hear all about it. I'm still amazed you agreed to do it in the first place."

"Me, too, but you know I really didn't have a choice except to leave Houston."

"Yes, you did," Ruth countered bluntly. "You could've opted to rent a cabin on the beach or used a lawyer friend's condo in New York to rest and relax. You didn't have to help me out."

"That's where you're wrong. One good deed deserves another. No matter what I do, it'll never be enough to repay you for what you did for me when I needed you the most four years ago."

"Let's not go down that road again. You don't owe me anything."

"Whatever."

"So how are things?"

Kelly brought her up-to-date as best she could, even telling her about Grant's troubles and their professional relationship—but not their personal one.

"I'm glad you're helping him. If he doesn't get out of that jam, it'll ruin him."

"If I have anything to do with it, he's not going to lose that timber."

"You go, girl. If anyone can straighten out those local yokels, it's you."

"Whoa, you're talking about your friends here."

Ruth laughed again. "Hey, the country has their share of idiots, too, you know."

"Oops, have to run," Kelly said with a chuckle. "Customers are coming. There's money to be made."

"I'm all for that. Talk to you later. But I'll see you sooner than later."

That conversation had taken place two days ago, and since then, Kelly had been working like crazy in the shop. It seemed like a new bout of cold weather had made people hungrier than usual, because business was better than ever.

It was after this morning's rush Kelly pondered the fact

she hadn't seen Grant since they'd had made love at his place. She hadn't even told him that Larry Ross had refused to take a DNA test. But she suspected he knew that wouldn't be news to Grant.

Still, it bothered her that she hadn't seen or talked to him.

Did he have regrets about his involvement with her? Probably not, because he knew she would be leaving soon. They had enjoyed a steamy night of lovemaking, which they both had needed, and that was that.

No regrets.

No commitments.

No future.

Perfect scenario.

She knew that was pure baloney, or she wouldn't be so anxious about his absence. And angry to boot. How dare he make love to her with such passion, then ignore her? She didn't need this aggravation in her life right now. She'd come here to de-stress rather than stress.

"Grr," Kelly muttered under her breath, just as the phone rang.

It was Maud. "Come over, Kelly. Right away!"

Maud was lying in a fetal position on the sofa in her cottage, out like a light.

Kelly added another blanket to the one already on the old woman before sitting back down in the chair near the fire. She had been with Maud for over an hour now, ever since they had returned from Dr. Graham's office.

Maud, of course, had pitched a fit at the thought of going to a doctor. But when Kelly had arrived at her house and found the old woman acting bizarre, as if she'd had a seizure or light stroke, grave concern had given Kelly the courage to force Maud into action.

"Am I going to die?"

Kelly whipped her gaze from the fire to Maud who had propped herself up on the pillow.

Pity washed though Kelly, but she didn't let it show. "Absolutely not. You're going to be just fine as long as you do what Dr. Graham tells you."

Maud frowned. "Tell me again what's wrong with me."

"Your blood sugar is out of whack. As long as you keep tabs on it and keep it in check, then you shouldn't have any more of these spells."

"Honest?"

"Honest." Kelly leaned forward and stared deeply into Maud's eyes. "Unless you disobey the doctor and eat your tea cakes."

Maud's chin wobbled just like it had at the doctor's office. "You mean I can never have another tea cake?"

"Never is a long time."

"But I'm a long time old," Maud countered.

Kelly smiled, leaned over and kissed her on the cheek. "Don't worry about that right now. Just behave yourself, and before long, I'll bet you'll can at least nibble on your delicacies. That's better than nothing."

Maud grabbed Kelly's hand and pulled it up to her bony cheek. "You're a good girl, Kelly Baker. I just wish you didn't have to leave us and go so far away. I'm going to miss you."

Surprisingly tears pooled in Kelly's eyes. "I'm going to miss you, too, Maud. A lot."

"Then don't go."

Kelly gently disengaged her hand. "I have to. My job, my life, my friends—they're all in Houston."

"What about me, Grant, Ruth? Aren't we your friends?"

Kelly's heart faltered. "Sure you are, and I plan to keep in touch."

"Hogwash."

Kelly was taken aback. "Be quiet and rest or I'm going to call Dr. Graham and tattle."

"Tattle all you want," Maud said with some of her spunk. "I want to talk to you about Grant."

Kelly kept her emotions under wraps. "There's nothing to talk about." She wished she meant that. There was actually lots to talk about, and that was the problem. But to dwell too much on Grant now would dredge up the precarious intimacy between them. She didn't want to go there.

"Of course there is." Maud struck out her tongue. "Only the both of you are apparently too stubborn to see it."

Kelly tried to downplay the seriousness of the moment by smiling, then saying, "You're just miffed because you want to play matchmaker and it isn't working.

"I may be old, young lady, but I'm not blind, nor am I deaf."

"I never said you were either."

"Sure you did," Maud said in an argumentative tone. "But if—"

"Thanks," Kelly interrupted with a smile. "How 'bout we change the subject."

Maud gave her a hard look, but then complied, especially as her eyelids were drooping. Kelly remained awhile longer, then finally slipped out of the cottage, her heart heavy.

* * *

The outdoors was Grant's salvation. Always had been and always would be. Tromping through the woods had a miraculous way of clearing his head and his soul. Today was no exception.

He still couldn't believe his equipment and crew remained idle. Even though it had only been a few days since he'd been shut down, to him it seemed like an eternity. He wasn't depressed or anxious. He was downright angry.

How had things gone from good to bad in such a short time? And not just on the work front.

Kelly.

He didn't know what to do about her. She had snuck in the back door of his heart and set up camp. He didn't love her. He wasn't there yet, not by any stretch of the imagination. But he sure cared about her and ached right now to make love to her again.

She was hot and willing, a rare combination in a woman. Soon, though, she would be gone for good. While that thought was unbearable, he had no solution to the problem.

Even if he'd wanted it, a long-distance romance never worked. He knew that when she left, things would be finished between them. She'd go back to her job in the big city while he stayed with his in the woods.

City girl and country boy? The two just weren't compatible. More than that, he wasn't interested in a relationship. He'd been alone so long now, he liked his life the way it was. He didn't see a need for a permanent change, except it sure was nice to have a beautiful woman in his bed.

Grant grimaced, then reminded himself there were

worse things than doing without—such as being saddled with a wife who was as different from him as day was from dark. But had he reached the time in his life where he might do something like fall for a woman?

He hoped the hell not.

Besides, there were lots of women willing to warm his bed. Problem was he hadn't cared enough to invite them into it. Then Kelly Baker came into his life.

Who would've ever guessed he'd become smitten with her?

"Damn," Grant muttered, as he continued his trek through the woods. Nearing the log set, he walked over to a large tree that was marked to be cut.

Suddenly he yearned to do just that. The very thought of operating equipment and harvesting trees was exhilarating. But just as quickly as his eagerness grew, it chilled. If he got caught, he'd end up in jail—something he could *not* afford in more ways than one.

Still Grant didn't move, continuing to lean against the tree. That was when he heard it. He shouted when something crashed through the underbrush in the opposite direction. His head and ears perked up. His eyes perused his surroundings, but he saw nothing. The forest became quiet again. Then he felt a searing pain in his shoulder.

Whipping his head down he watched in horror as blood saturated his thick shirt. Grant's stomach roiled and he slid to his knees.

He'd been shot.

Fifteen

Kelly couldn't stop pacing the floor in the surgery waiting room. Her legs simply wouldn't cooperate and remain still enough for her to sit down.

"You're going to wear yourself and the carpet out, you know," Pete drawled. He was kicked back in a chair, his legs sprawled out in front of him.

There were other people in the room, but as a whole the place was fairly empty, which gave Kelly the freedom she needed to pace.

"I know," she admitted, pausing for a moment, "but my insides feel like they're turned inside out."

Pete raised his eyebrows, as if to ask what was going on with her and Grant. He was far too intuitive, so she'd best be on guard. But that was hard when she was so obviously anxious.

When an excited man had come through the door of the coffee shop an hour ago and announced there had been an accident in the woods, that Grant Wilcox had been shot, Kelly took action.

She had told Doris she was headed to the hospital in Wellington, then she'd called Pete. She had arrived at the E.R. just as Grant's gurney was being wheeled down the hall toward surgery.

When Grant had seen her, he'd said to the attendant, "Wait a minute."

Feeling as though her heart was going to literally jump out of her chest, Kelly had stopped beside the stretcher. Before she could speak, however, she'd had to force air into her lungs. "What…what happened?"

Despite the pain she knew he was in, his gaze on her had softened. "Some idiot shot me in the shoulder, which is no big deal."

She gasped. "No big deal! How can you say that when you're headed to surgery?"

"It could have been my heart."

While that sobering comment certainly put things in perspective, Kelly still didn't see getting shot as minor. Men and their logic.

"Ma'am, we have to go."

Grant had reached out, grabbed her hand and peered deep into her eyes.

She'd squeezed his hand tightly, then let it go. "I'll be waiting."

"I'll see you soon." He'd winked.

By the time she made it to the waiting area, Kelly's throat was too full to speak. And there sat Pete, who merely looked at her through inquisitive eyes. Neither said anything. If she had wanted to, she could've made her way to a corner and let the tears flow, but that wouldn't do any good.

Grant was going to be just fine, she told herself with firm conviction. He'd be out of surgery in no time and would be as good as new.

The idea that her stomach was a tight ball of fear was ridiculous. Suddenly she froze again.

Love.

In connection with Grant? No way. That could not be. It wasn't possible. She couldn't have been so foolish as to have fallen in love with this woodsman.

Only she knew that she had. Before Kelly's knees gave way, she eased into the nearest chair, which just happened to be next to Pete.

"Thank goodness," he said with a halfhearted grin, "you're finally sitting down."

She tried to smile, but it wouldn't happen.

Pete reached over and awkwardly patted her hand. "He's going to be fine. He's a tough old bird. It'll take more than a bullet to the shoulder to get him down."

She nodded, unable to share with him her heart's secret—the real reason she was so upset. She'd fallen in love with a man with whom she had no future.

"Now, if he loses his right to cut the timber on Holland's land—" Pete's voice broke off and a pained expression crossed his face. "That would be worse than him getting shot in the shoulder."

Kelly rallied. "He's not going to lose his timber."

"How can you be so sure?"

"I think Judge Winston will do the right thing."

Pete's thin lips turned downward. "Man, I hope so. I still can't believe that bastard Ross—" He stopped and cleared his throat. "Uh, excuse me, ma'am."

Kelly shook her head. "No apology necessary. Remember I work with a group of male attorneys. Trust me, I've heard worse."

"Trust me, I could have called him worse, too."

They both smiled, then fell silent again.

"Don't you think the doctors have had time to finish working on him?"

"Nah," Pete said, crossing his sprawled legs. "By the time they prep him and all, it takes more time than you think."

Kelly knew that, having had more experiences in surgery waiting rooms with family and friends. But this was different. This was the man she had just realized she loved.

Her stomach somersaulted, and she felt sick. What was she going to do? *Nothing,* her heart cried. What could she do? The answer was clear. She would go on with her life just as he would go on with his.

Doing different things in different places.

"You care about him, don't you?"

She saw no reason to hedge any longer. "Yes, I do."

"I'm glad. He's been alone too long."

An alarm went off inside her head. "Look, don't think—"

Pete held up his hand, stopping her words. "I don't think anything, ma'am, so don't go making a mountain out of a molehill."

"Call me Kelly."

"Okay, Kelly. All I'm saying is that since you've been here, I've seen a difference in Grant—a good difference, I might add. If that good only lasts a little while, that's better than nothing."

"I still can't believe he never married." She shouldn't be delving into Grant's life behind his back, especially under these circumstances. But despite Grant's explanation, it still mystified her that he'd remained single all these years.

Pete smiled. "He's too damn picky. When it comes to women, that is."

"That doesn't tell me a lot," Kelly said, making small talk in hopes of keeping her mind off of what was happening in surgery.

"He likes living in the sticks."

"Then that's where he should stay."

"And he sure as hell likes his independence."

"He should keep it." Kelly said those words with a sinking heart, then hated herself for feeling this way. Whatever she'd been fishing for hadn't materialized. Grant was who he was, and he wasn't about to change.

Certainly not for her.

They heard someone clear his throat behind them, and Kelly and Pete whipped around. "Ah, Amos," Pete said, rising. "Come join us."

Instantly, Kelly knew who this tall stringbean of a man was. He'd been in the coffee shop a couple of times. She stood and, out of courtesy, shook his hand, though her heart was pounding hard.

Kelly didn't think he'd made an appearance for appearance sake. She knew he had something to say. He looked uncomfortable, fiddling with the hat he held in his hand. He seemed to avoid looking at her, choosing to keep his gaze glued on Pete.

"Sheriff, was Grant's shooting deliberate?"

Kelly's blunt question seemed to take both men aback.

Pete's eyes narrowed, while Amos shifted from foot to foot. Then the sheriff's face cleared and he actually smiled, which seemed to tempered his nervousness.

"Uh, we're not sure, ma'am."

Kelly's mouth turned dust-dry, and her eyes widened in horror. "You mean…" Her voice shriveled into nothing.

"I figured it was some damn hog hunter, or a kid taking target practice," Pete commented in a grave voice. "The idea that someone might intentionally shoot at Grant never entered my mind."

Kelly let out her pent-up breath and shook her head, still too horrified to speak. Things like this just didn't happen to people she knew, especially someone she cared about, for heaven's sake."

After licking her dry lips, she said, "He could have easily been—" She broke off, unable to say the word *killed*.

"We know, ma'am," the sheriff said softly, respectfully. "It's a God thing. That's the way I see it." Changing the subject, he added, "Let Grant know the investigation's taking top priority."

"If someone did take a shot at him," Pete said in a harsh tone, "I pity the poor dumb son of a bitch when you find him. Grant will be out for blood."

"Look," Amos said, rubbing his chin, "we're doing a thorough investigation. We will find out who's responsible. As soon as we know something, we'll be back in touch." He paused and cleared his throat again. "Meanwhile, how's Grant?"

"We don't know yet," Pete said before Kelly could respond.

Amos left shortly thereafter, leaving behind a tense silence.

Kelly's eyes kept veering to the O.R. door and she was finally rewarded. A tall, bald man dressed in surgery greens entered the room.

"Ms. Baker?"

She and Pete both stood expectantly.

"I'm Dr. Carpenter, and Grant's fine. We removed the bullet without a problem." He paused and wiped his forehead. "He did, however, lose quite a bit of blood so I'm keeping him overnight."

"You mean he might have gone home otherwise?" Kelly asked in an astounded tone.

"Home, yes, only we don't recommend he go alone." The doctor looked troubled. "When he awakens, something tells me he's not going to like that."

Pete chuckled. "You can say that again. He'll be pitching a fit to get out of here."

"May I see him?" Kelly asked.

Dr. Carpenter nodded. "He's in recovery, but because it's not real busy, I'll let you sit with him."

"Thank you, sir," Kelly said with heartfelt relief, even though she realized she was adding another nail to her emotional coffin.

Leaving Pete behind, she followed the doctor.

"It's about damn time I'm getting out of this place."

"You only had to say overnight," Kelly said in a soothing, even tone, trying to calm Grant.

"That was one night too many."

Kelly wanted to tell him to stop his bellyaching, but she kept silent. She knew the pain medication had probably worn off and he was feeling discomfort. That would make anyone grouchy, especially someone who wasn't used to pain.

Once they were in her vehicle, Kelly turned on the engine then didn't move. Grant faced her and said, "Pete told me my getting shot might not have been accidental."

"That's right," she stated, telling him about the conversation with the sheriff.

"If you ask me, that's a stretch."

"Amos didn't sound that sure."

"Hunters, legal and illegal, have always been a burr in a forester's butt," Grant said. "We've learned to keep our distance."

"So you think it was a hunter?"

"Or a kid playing with his daddy's gun."

"That's what Pete said."

They were both quiet for a moment, then Grant added in a grave tone, "Are you thinking what I'm thinking?"

She cut a look at him. "That Larry Ross might be the culprit?"

Grant's expression was grim. "Yep. We're on the same page. If it was deliberate, then he's the only one I can think of who would benefit from my demise."

"But when you really think about it rationally," Kelly said, "that's ludicrous. First, what would he have to gain, and second, how could he expect to get away with it? I'm sure he's the number-one suspect."

Cold fury glinted in Grant's eyes. "If it wasn't an accident, then he sure as hell is mine."

"You'll just have to be patient and let the law work."

"And not take matters into my own hands." Grant's voice was icy-cold. "Is that what you're saying?"

"Absolutely, but then you know that."

"Don't be too sure." Grant paused for a moment, then changed the subject, his tone becoming thick and husky. "I understand I'm going home with you."

Kelly's hand stilled on the gearshift as desire leaped in his eyes. She swallowed, then said in a slightly unsteady voice, "Let's get two things straight—its not *my* home and *you're* going straight to the spare bedroom."

"Aw, shucks," he said.

She glared at him before backing out of the parking lot.

"Just because my arm's out of commission doesn't mean anything else is."

"Speaking of your arm, how is it?

"Believe it or not, it doesn't hurt all that much. In fact, I can even move it up and down without much pain."

"Still, you don't have complete control of it," Kelly stressed. "My fear is that one wrong move could rip open the stitches. Then you'd be in a heap of trouble."

Grant shrugged, his mouth in a pout. "I think you're overreacting, but go on and drive. I'm just jerking your chain. I promise I'll be a good boy."

He paused and she felt his smoldering gaze on her. "But I won't promise for how long."

Deciding it was best not to respond to that, Kelly steered the car into the street. "I need to stop by the coffee shop for a second and check on things."

"Take your time. I'm not going anywhere."

"By the way, have you heard anything from the sheriff?"

"Nope, not yet. But if I don't real soon, I'll be rattling his chain."

Kelly tended to business then, fifteen minutes later, drove to Ruth's driveway. She and Grant were about to go inside when she heard another vehicle pull in behind her. She turned around, and her jaw dropped.

John Billingsly? What on earth is he doing here?

"Who is that?" Grant asked in a slightly irritated tone, as if he realized something was not quite right.

"It's…my boss."

Sixteen

She was stunned to see John Billingsly in Lane, Texas, especially on a Monday, one of the busiest days at the firm. The fact that Grant was standing next to her giving John the once-over through narrowed eyes didn't help any.

Clearing her throat, Kelly made the appropriate introductions. Then John, looking slightly uncomfortable, said, "It appears I've come at a bad time."

"Not as far as I'm concerned," Grant said in an offhand manner, waving his good arm. "I'll leave you two alone." He paused, facing John. "Nice to meet you."

John nodded. "Same here."

Once Grant had disappeared inside, Kelly simply stared at her boss, thinking how tired he looked. Even so, that didn't detract from his handsomeness. He was tall, with broad shoulders, a thatch of silver hair and a killer smile.

She couldn't forget about that. Or what a great voice he had, which was one of the reasons he commanded so much respect in the courtroom.

"So what brings you here?" she asked. Then, as if she needed to qualify that question so he wouldn't think she was rude, she added, "Of course, I'm glad to see you."

John gave her a half smile. "I'm sure you are, but not as glad as I'd like you to be."

Kelly flushed. "I don't know what you mean."

"Oh, I think you do." John nodded toward the door. "What's with him?"

"He's a friend who just got out of the hospital."

John's eyes probed, as if searching for the whole truth.

She ignored that gaze and said, "You're actually a sight for sore eyes, as I'm dying to know how things are at the firm." She hoped her tone was cool and even because inside she was shaking.

"Then let's go somewhere and talk. Lunch, perhaps. I want to know how you're doing, then I want to bring you up-to-date on the firm. We have a couple of cases coming up that have your name on them."

"That's great."

He raised thick eyebrows. "Is that all you have to say?"

Kelly did some mental tap dancing while sweat pooled under her breasts. "I'd love to visit with you over lunch, only now's not a good time.

"Are you due back at the shop?"

"Actually, it's closed today."

John lifted his eyebrows in question, as if to ask why she couldn't leave. When she didn't answer, he murmured, "Looks like I shot myself in the foot by coming without calling first. I'm assuming it has something to do with the guy in there." He inclined his head toward the door.

"That's only partly true," Kelly said with conviction. "How about we sit on the porch swing and talk?"

After all, it was a nice day, and she couldn't just send him back without spending some time with him. The fact that he'd come to see her was a big deal, and she had to treat it as such. Her job was her life; if her boss wanted to see her, then she'd be a fool not to accommodate him. Besides, Grant could take care of himself for a while.

Once they were seated, John smiled at her. "You seem good."

"I am," she answered, with a sincere smile of her own. "You were right. I needed to get away. Only I have a confession to make."

"Oh?"

"I've been doing a little work."

"On a case?"

She nodded, then explained.

"You'll get no flack from me. I think it's great that you're dabbling in the law again and feeling good about it."

She gave him a big smile. "I'm so glad you approve, even though I haven't won the case yet."

"You will," he said with conviction.

"Thanks. Your confidence makes me feel even better."

"So when can we expect you back?"

"Just as soon as my cousin returns."

A relieved expression crossed John's face, making him look less tired. "What about him?"

Kelly didn't pretend to misunderstand the emphasis

behind this question, though she wasn't about to answer it. "What *about* him?"

John merely shrugged. "Okay, so you don't want to talk about him. I can accept that."

"While you're at it, accept that I can't wait to get back to work."

John reached out and squeezed her hand. "Everyone misses you, including myself. We can't wait to have you return."

"Thank," Kelly said, feeling tears gather in her eyes. "You don't know how much that means to me."

He rose. "I'm going now, but we'll talk later."

"Thanks for coming. I'm just sorry—"

John held up his hand. "No apology necessary. Again, I should've called first." He smiled with a wink. "I'll see you soon."

Kelly smiled in return, giving him a thumbs-up. "You can count on that."

She waited until he was back in his BMW and on the street before she made her way into the house. Closing the door, where she paused and leaned back against it. That was when she noticed Grant hadn't made it to Ruth's spare bedroom, but instead had crashed on the sofa. He appeared to be sound asleep.

She fixed her gaze on him, thinking how good he looked, especially now that the deep lines around his eyes and mouth were relaxed. Yet she sensed a vulnerability about him that tore at her heart. Between his job situation and this mishap, he was mentally and physically stressed. Even though he hadn't let on, she knew he'd probably like to bite a tenpenny nail in two.

She was tempted to walk over and rub Grant's cheek with the back of her hand for the sheer pleasure of simply touching him. Every time she saw him she *wanted* to touch him. But since that kind of "touching" had no future, she kept her hands to herself.

Especially since their lives remained worlds apart and always would.

Pulling her thoughts off Grant before she did something she would regret, Kelly forced herself to think about John and what had just taken place between them.

She remained a bit shell-shocked from his unexpected appearance. While she had wanted to spend time with him, she hadn't felt good about leaving Grant, thinking of the doctor's comments. For a second, she'd actually been pulled in two directions. She wasn't sure she'd made the right choice, either.

Now, as she shoved away from the door and made her way quietly past the sofa so as not to awaken Grant, she took a deep breath, trying to calm her rattled nerves. Why did life have to be so complicated? She was at the end of the sofa when her hand was grabbed.

Wide-eyed, she swung around and saw that Grant was sitting up, her hand clasped in his.

"You…you startled me," she said in a halting voice. "I thought you were asleep."

"I was just resting."

Their gazes locked together like magnets. Then he peered down at her left hand, and back up at her face. "I expected you to be gone with your boyfriend."

Tugging her hand free, she shoved it into her jean pocket. "He's not my boyfriend," she said tersely. "He's my boss. But then you know that."

"He's got a thing for you."

"So what if he does?"

Now why had she said that? Perhaps to make Grant jealous? For what purpose? Grant didn't love her. He felt only lust. Without commitment. And right or wrong, she had enjoyed every minute of being the focus of that lust.

"Ah, so you're keeping the poor bastard dangling."

She saw red. "What I'm doing is none of your business."

"You're damn straight, it's not," he agreed in a harsh tone as he got to his feet. "Nothing you do is my business and nothing I do is yours." Their eyes met again in a clash of wills. "Right?"

"Right," she said defiantly, holding herself together by a mere thread.

"I feel like hell. I'm going to bed."

When she heard the door to the guest bedroom close, Kelly sat on the sofa, her insides churning. If she ever thought he loved her, his words had just proved her dead wrong.

She grabbed a pillow, buried her face in it and sobbed.

"You look all tuckered out, girlie."

"I am, Maud."

"Before I came, I took some tea cakes out of the oven. Why don't you come by and have some?"

"Thanks, but no thanks. I'm going home to soak my tired bones in the tub. I'll take a rain check, though."

"You sure? I'll be glad to go home, get them and bring them to you."

"Don't you dare. I'm simply too pooped to eat anything right now."

"Okey-dokey. I'll see you later, then."

Thank goodness Maud hadn't probed. Usually, she wouldn't take no for an answer. Now that she had gone, Kelly breathed a sigh of relief, thankful the day was over. Business had remained exceptionally good. People had been in and out all day.

Except Grant.

She hadn't seen him in a couple of days. The night he'd spent in Ruth's spare room had been a short one. She'd awakened at five o'clock the next morning to check on him only to find him gone. She had no idea when he'd gotten up and left. She needed to talk to him, too, as she'd gotten the court hearing moved to the day after tomorrow.

As a result of his absence, Kelly didn't know which she wanted to do more—shake him or kiss him. She couldn't stop thinking about that hot night of passion they shared. But it was best this way, she knew. Best that he stayed away. Best that he was in no condition to touch her.

"We're leaving, Kelly," Doris said, poking her head through the swinging door.

"Me, too. See you guys in the morning."

Kelly had the door locked and was about to get in her car when Grant's pickup pulled up beside her.

"Climb in and let's go for a ride."

The idea that he was ordering her around didn't even register. The fact that he was driving did, however. "What are you doing behind the wheel?"

"I got one good hand."

"Grant Wilcox, you're nuts. You could have a wreck and kill yourself or someone else."

"Are you coming?"

"No."

"Please."

When he looked at her like that, her good sense seemed to go by the wayside, and she couldn't deny him anything, much less time. They had so little of it left that each moment seemed precious.

"Only if you let me drive."

"Have you ever driven a truck?"

"No."

He laughed, got out, then made a sweeping gesture with his good arm. "It's all yours."

Once Kelly got behind the wheel, she simply sat there, feeling his eyes on her. When she faced him, a teasing smile radiated from his lips and eyes. "It's easy driving, actually. It's just like a car, so let's go."

After adjusting the seat and the rearview mirror, she started the engine.

"Hang a right here," Grant said when she had maneuvered onto the street. "We're headed to Wellington. I have a piece of equipment in a mechanic shop that I need to check on."

"That reminds me," Kelly said. "We go to court day after tomorrow on the DNA test."

"That's great. I just know that bastard Ross is lying through his pearly whites."

"What if he's not?"

"Then I'm sunk," Grant said flatly. "My only recourse is to turn around and sue Holland to get my money back."

"Unless the judge orders Holland to give Ross his fair share of the timber money."

"Can he do that?"

"Judges are little gods." Kelly smiled without humor. "They can do anything they want to."

Grant raised his head. "Then let us pray."

The rest of the drive passed in silence, though Kelly was conscious of Grant occupying the seat next to her. She ached to touch him. The few times their gazes tangled, she saw the same smoldering desire in his. She simply gripped the steering wheel tighter and told herself to keep her distance, that dallying with him would only leave her hurting.

Once they reached the city limits of Wellington, Grant directed her to the equipment dealer. She waited in the truck while he went inside and attended to business.

"It's not ready yet," he said, climbing in the cab. "Which is probably a good thing, because it's going to cost megabucks to get it out. Bucks that I don't have right now."

It was on the tip of her tongue to say that she'd loan him the money, but Kelly thought better of it after looking at his grim features. Her instinct told her he wouldn't accept money from her.

"Where to now?" she asked. "Back to Lane?"

"Yep, unless you want to grab a bit of early dinner."

"I'd rather head back."

"That's fine with me."

They were just out of Wellington, on a side road when she saw the most beautiful house she could have imagined. Constructed of white stone, it nestled among huge trees and lush shrubs, though it didn't look unkempt. On the contrary, it looked peaceful and inviting. So intrigued was Kelly with it, that she actually slowed the truck.

"What a lovely place," she said in awe.

"You gotta be kidding."

Kelly stopped the truck and faced him. "What's that supposed to mean?"

He shrugged. "I'm just surprised that you'd think any house outside of a subdivision was pretty."

"Well, this is about as close to country living as I'd like."

"Even at that, I doubt you'd be happy. People from the city just don't belong here."

Guess that told her. Kelly's eyes flashed fire at her dismissal. "Do you intentionally try to make me angry, or does it just come naturally?"

He swore. "I don't think that calls for an answer."

The remainder of the drive was done in hostile silence. When they arrived at Ruth's place, Kelly bounded out of the truck and made her way inside. Grant grabbed her arm and swung her around to face him.

"Look, I'm sorry. I should've kept my mouth shut."

"Yes, you should have."

"Would you buy it if I told you I was under a lot of stress?"

"No."

"Didn't think you would." He rubbed his jaw. "Would you buy this? What if I told you I wanted to make you hate me so that I wouldn't want to kiss you every time you came near me?"

Blood beat with hammer force in her ears.

"Oh, to hell with it," Grant muttered, placing his good hand against her shoulder and backing her against the wall, his breathing harsh and erratic.

Within seconds, he was grinding his lips to hers.

If she hadn't been propped up, she would have melted into a puddle on the floor. Yet she gave back as good as she got, wrapping her arms around his neck, reveling in the feelings he evoked in her.

"God, I want you so much it's killing me." His voice sounded desperate.

"I want you, too," she whispered with an ache, loving him with a full and complete heart.

"I mean here." His eyes, staring into hers, were as hot as his lips had been. "Now."

"Now? What…what about your shoulder?"

"You let me take care of that," he growled.

Without further words and without taking her eyes off him, she unzipped his jeans, releasing his erection. He in turn shoved her blue jean skirt up and jerked her thong down. Kelly stepped out of them just as his strong hand cupped one cheek of her buttocks.

As if she knew exactly what he had in mind, she circled his neck with her arms. Then using all her strength, she sprang up and clasped her legs around him.

Entering her swift and hard, he groaned, "Oh, Kelly, Kelly."

Seventeen

She leaned over him, her fingers delving into the hairs on his chest, playing in them. At some point they had ended up in Kelly's bed, though she had no recollection of the particulars. After that heady session against the wall, her mind had gone on hiatus.

Only not for long. As soon as they reached the bed, their lovemaking started all over again. At first she was mindful of his shoulder, but it became apparent that his wound didn't diminish Grant's passion. It was as if they couldn't get enough of each other's bodies. She wanted him with the same intensity as he wanted her.

What had come over her? True, she was in love with Grant. But then, she'd been in love with her husband, too. With Grant it was different. He tapped into a part of herself she hadn't known existed—a wild side.

Exciting?

Yes.

Crazy?

Yes?

Dangerous?

Yes.

Permanent?

No.

Even though her heart wrenched at that thought, Kelly still didn't want to move away from his warm body, didn't want *not* to touch him. Her fingers were having a field day running over his chest and stomach.

And lower.

Groaning, Grant looked up at her with fire in his eyes. She was resting on an elbow, and knew her own eyes burned with that same fire. Neither of them bothered to turn off the lamp in the bedroom. Not so with Eddie. Their lovemaking had been done in the dark.

"What are you thinking about?" Grant asked in his low, brusque voice.

"Eddie. My husband."

Grant hesitated, then asked in a resigned voice, "What about him?"

"Although we really loved each other, our lovemaking was never wild or passionate. That's so clear to me now."

Grant's eyes darkened, then he said, "Thank you for telling me that. You have no idea how humble or how good that makes me feel." He paused to kiss her. "I've never made love to any woman like I've made love to you. The spark, fire, whatever you want to call it, just wasn't there." He paused again. "Maybe that's why I never married."

Those last words hung in the air for a long moment, creating a stifling tension.

Feeling sad for a reason she refused to admit, Kelly replaced her fingers with her lips, first tonguing his nipples until they were as rigid as hers.

"Mmm, that feels so good," he said in a guttural tone.

"This should feel even better." Using her tongue, she moved lower, down the middle of his flat stomach to his belly button,where she delved and sucked.

He moaned and squirmed as she moved even farther south. When she reached his swollen manhood, she paused and looked at him, gauging his reaction. He had raised himself onto his elbows and stared back at her, his eyes heated and glazed.

"It's…it's your call," he said in a croaking voice.

She lowered her lips onto the soft head and sucked. And sucked some more.

"Oh, Kelly," he cried, "yes, yes."

She climbed over him, sinking onto that hard shaft. Shortly, their moans turned into cries that filled the room.

How could she ever let him go? That question that went through Kelly's mind when she finally lay beside him, exhausted but satisfied, and happy beyond her wildest dreams.

"Kelly, it's John."

Her heart raced. "It's good to hear from you again."

"Same here. Having said that, I'll come straight to the point."

"Why not?" she replied a bit breathlessly. Something was up. She could tell by his crisp tone.

"You remember me mentioning the firm had a couple of cases with your name on them?

"Of course."

"Well, we're about to take them on, and we want you in on the sessions from the get-go, which means we need you here ASAP."

"Oh, John, I'd like nothing better than to say I could leave now, but I can't, though I am expecting my cousin back any day now."

A deep sigh filtered through the line. "We'll hold off as long as we can." He paused. "How's your case going?"

"It should be resolved soon."

"Good. So it won't prevent your returning to Houston when your cousin gets back." He paused again, this time longer. "You remember our talk about a partnership?"

How could she forget *that?* "I do."

"Well, if you ace these new cases, you'll be a shoo-in."

"I don't know what to say, except thanks." Kelly heart was really racing now.

John chuckled. "That's enough. Keep me informed."

"I will, and thanks again for calling."

Once she'd replaced the receiver, Kelly laughed and hollered, "Yes!"

She had made her career her life, and it was finally paying off. But then, just as quickly as that excitement flared, it died. She sand into the nearest chair, her legs like jelly.

Grant.

She would be leaving Grant, wouldn't be seeing him anymore, wouldn't be trading insults with him anymore. *Wouldn't be making love to him anymore.* That couldn't be, not when she loved him.

Yet what choice did she have? He'd never said he loved her and even if he did, a future between them was impossible. He wanted one thing, and she another. And those "wants" were as far apart as the wealth of the queen of England and a starving artist.

Thinking of Grant made Kelly long for him. He hadn't been in the coffee shop all day, nor had he called her. She'd been so busy she really hadn't had time to dwell on the fact, but now that it was closing time and the afternoon loomed empty before her, she wanted to hear from him.

She wanted to see him.

Each time they were together, she fell deeper in love. The thought of leaving him appalled her; the thought of remaining appalled her, as well.

"Yahoo, toots!"

Stunned, Kelly swung around and watched as Ruth strode toward her, arms outstretched. Kelly couldn't believe her eyes. Fate. That was the only thing to which she could attribute this unexpected twist.

"When did you get home?" Kelly asked, laughing as she returned Ruth's bear hug.

"Actually, I haven't been home." Ruth's eyes gazed about, seeming to soak up everything. "This is the first place I hit."

"It's so good to see you."

Ruth giggled. "I can imagine."

"I didn't mean it that way," Kelly said seriously. "Believe me or not, this has truly been a fun experience."

"Yeah, right."

Kelly shook her head. "I'm not pulling your leg."

"Trust me, I'm glad. I was afraid you wouldn't speak to me again."

Kelly rolled her eyes. "I just hope you won't think I've destroyed your business with my ineptness."

"Hasn't happened," Ruth declared. "If you can pour coffee and sling hash, you can run this place." She chuckled, her tall, big-boned frame shaking all over and her green eyes twinkling. "Even though we both know you've never done either."

Kelly placed her hands on her hips as though insulted. "I'll have you know I've done both. Once upon a time, that is."

"Hey, I'm just teasing," Ruth said, "but you know that. Come on, let's go home and catch up on everything."

"I can't wait."

"Kelly?"

She swung back around and saw Doris holding the phone. "It's a Mr. Mangum for you."

Kelly's heart skipped a beat.

"Who's that?" Ruth asked, as if sensing Kelly's reaction.

"I'll explain later. You go on and I'll follow."

"You take your call, and I'll see to the shop," Ruth said.

Kelly closed the door to the tiny office and reached for the receiver. For Grant, this was the moment of truth. "Hello, Mr. Mangum."

"I thought I might find you here."

Grant removed his hat and strode toward Kelly, leaving Pete fiddling with a piece of equipment. "Hey, babe," he said, leaning over and kissing her.

Slightly shocked at familiarity, especially in front of Pete, Kelly felt color seep into her cheeks.

Grant chuckled. "It amazes me that you can still blush after what we've shared."

"Stop it," she muttered, though a smile lurked around her lips. "Pete might hear you."

"Nah, he's too busy playing with that loader." Grant paused. "Now, me, I'd rather play with you."

"You're impossible," Kelly retorted.

"But you love it, only you won't admit it."

"You're right, I won't."

Grant pulled a face, then grinned. "What brings you here?"

"Good news."

Grant's body stilled. "Go on."

"Larry Ross took the DNA test and failed it."

"Glory be!" Grant shouted. He tossed his hard hat in the air, then grabbed Kelly and swung her around and around. When he put her back down, she was so dizzy she clung to him.

"You used both your arms," she said in amazement.

"That's right. Happiness will do that to a guy. Plus, my arm hardly bothers me at all."

"Dr. Carpenter must be one good surgeon."

"Grant grinned. "Must be."

Pete joined them, his gaze fixed on Grant. "What the hell's going on here? I heard you hollering like a banshee."

"We're good to go." Grant slapped Pete on his arm. "At last."

Pete whooped. "You mean we can start the engines?"

"That's exactly what it means," Kelly said, laughing now that she had pulled herself back together.

"Thank you so much, ma'am," Pete said bowing in front of her.

"Get out of here," she said through her laughter.

"You want me to notify the crew?" Pete asked Grant.

"Tell 'em to report to work first thing tomorrow morning."

"Will do."

Once Pete had walked off, Grant's features sobered. "Thanks. You know I mean that."

"I know you do."

"So how did you pull it off?"

"Apparently Ross got in some financial trouble due to gambling. Because he needed money, and because he was so sure he was a legal heir, he agreed to the test." She smiled up at Grant. "As they say, the rest is history."

"Of your making," he said. "If you hadn't pushed for the DNA test, I'd still be sitting on the sidelines." He reached out, grabbed her, pulled her against him and kissed her hard and deep. "That's my thanks in action."

Breathlessly, Kelly pulled back and was about to speak when Pete cut in. "Aw, come on, you two. Give me a break."

They both shot him a grin, which he returned. "So we got Ross on the DNA, but what about your shoulder? I'm still not sure that SOB isn't responsible for that."

Grant's features turned serious. "My gut tells me he's not that stupid, but then what do I know? When I leave here, I'm stopping by to see Amos."

It was then that his cell phone rang. He looked at the caller ID and raised his eyebrows, then said, "Hey, Sheriff, your ears must've been burning." Grant listened for a minute then added, "Yeah, okay. I'll be there shortly."

"So?" Kelly and Pete asked almost simultaneously.

"Ross has been cleared. He has an ironclad alibi for the time of the shooting."

"Damn," Pete muttered.

Kelly looked at Grant. "Then who shot you? Does Amos know?"

"Yep, but he wants to talk to me about it in person."

"At least the mystery's solved," Pete said. "Just let me know the details."

When Pete had driven off, Kelly turned to Grant and said, "We need to talk."

"You bet we do. How 'bout I cook steaks tonight and you come over?"

Kelly's stomach flipped. "I'll be there."

Everything was as perfect as Grant could possibly make it. He had cleaned the house and bought flowers for the rustic dining room table. Although they looked a bit out of place, just stuck in a vase, he was proud of them, nonetheless.

The salad was made. The beer was iced down. The wine was chilled. The potatoes were baking. The steaks ready to throw on the grill.

And he was ready to see Kelly. Now and forever.

Grant's gut twisted at the word *forever.* He didn't mean that. Yes, he did, his conscience taunted back. Had he fallen in love? While that thought panicked him, he wanted to know the answer. For him, love and lust were so closely entwined it was hard to know which was which.

God, he was sweating as if he'd been blazing a trail in the woods. He had to do better than this, or she'd think he'd lost it.

A knock on the door saved him.

He opened it and Kelly walked straight into his arms,

holding on to him as though she'd never let him go, which was a-okay with him.

Finally, he pushed her back, and smiled down at her, then kissed her softly. "Good evening."

"Good evening to you," she said in a slightly winded tone.

Something was wrong; he sensed it deep in his gut. But he wouldn't push her. She'd tell him when she was ready.

"Looks like we're celebrating," she commented, moving deeper into the room.

He gave her a sheepish smile. "Pretty pitiful, aren't they?"

"If you're talking about the flowers, I think they're lovely."

"We both know that's not true, but it sounds good, anyway."

"You're impossible," Kelly declared, shaking her head.

"Sit down," Grant said with a nervousness that stunned and annoyed him. "You want wine or beer?"

"Neither right now."

His eyebrows shot up.

"I'd like to hear what Amos said. About who shot you, to be exact."

Grant shook his head. "You won't believe what I'm about to tell you."

"Sure I will. I'm an attorney, remember?"

"Some sixteen-year-old kid decided to take his rifle and do some shooting. He borrowed his dad's truck and wound up on Holland's land. When he saw a wild hog, he stalked it.

"To make a long story short, when he finally got the opportunity to shoot, he fired, but missed. Of course, the hog took off, crashing through the underbrush. That's when I hollered and the kid got scared and ran like hell.

"He was so scared that he ran into a tree, and that's what brought about the confession. He had to tell his parents about the dent in the truck and trespassing on Holland's land.

"A couple of days later his dad heard about someone getting shot. The parents then put two and two together and figured out what had happened. Voilà! Today they appeared at Amos's office."

"He could've killed you," Kelly said in a solemn tone.

"I know. Amos asked if I wanted to press charges."

"Are you?"

"Nah. The poor kid is already scared out of his wits, knowing he hurt someone. It was an accident. Plus he has his parents to contend with, and Amos said they were not happy."

"Kids," Kelly said, shaking her head. "But at least, as Amos said, the mystery is solved. And now you're well on the road to recovery."

Grant gave her a leering grin. "You got that right, which means I can ravish you with all my limbs intact."

"We need to talk first."

"I thought that's what we just did."

"About something else."

"Fine. So talk."

"Ruth's back."

Grant visibly stiffened. "As of when?"

"This afternoon around closing time."

He forced a smile. "That's good. I'm sure you're both glad about that."

A disturbing silence followed.

"You might not need anything to drink," Grant said at last, "but I sure do." He strode into the kitchen and grabbed a beer, sucked half of it down before removing the bottle from his lips.

Kelly had followed him into the kitchen, her eyes and face serious. This time his heart twisted. "When are you leaving?" he asked.

"Soon."

"I figured as much, since I've learned to read you pretty well." Grant paused. "Before you say anything else, I want to ask you something."

"Go ahead."

"Do you think there's a chance that we, you and me, could have a future together?" When she opened her mouth to say something, he raised his hand. "I know we're from two different worlds, as corny as that sounds, and I know we're as different as two people can be." He paused and rubbed the back of his neck. "But hell, those differences make life exciting, make relationships exciting."

"Grant…"

He ignored her. "If we were all alike, how boring would that be?"

"What are you saying?" Kelly asked in a small voice, her eyes scouring his face.

"Bottom line. Will you stay awhile longer…with me? Let's see where this thing goes with us."

"Grant. John called. From Houston."

The next silence was long and stifling.

"Are you going to say anything?" Kelly asked at last.

"I've had my say. It's your turn now."

"My firm wants me back ASAP."

Though Kelly didn't say anything else, Grant could tell that she was struggling. God, he wanted to hold her. In fact, he wanted to grab her, kiss her, tell her he loved her, then beg her not to go.

Instead, he stood unmoving and mute.

"And I feel like I owe them, and I owe myself. So I'm leaving tomorrow."

Grant gave her a long, hard look, then said in a drawling tone, "I guess that pretty much says it all."

"That doesn't mean—"

Grant shook his head. "Oh, I know what it means. You've decided to haul it back to Houston." He shrugged. "And I'm not about to try and change your mind."

Her face went white. "Are you telling me it's over."

"You're the big-shot lawyer. Can't you figure that out?"

They stared at each other long and hard.

"You're also telling me I should leave now, aren't you?" Kelly could barely get the question past the lump in her throat.

"Under the circumstances, I think that's probably a good idea."

Blinking back tears, Kelly pivoted on her heel and walked out the door, closing it softly behind her.

Cursing, Grant threw the bottle of beer at the fireplace. When the glass shattered everywhere, he didn't so much as flinch.

Eighteen

"Have I told you lately how proud I am of you?"

"Every day."

John smiled before plopping down in a chair in front of Kelly's desk. "I just want to make sure you're aware of what a great job you're doing and how much the firm appreciates it."

"I know, and I appreciate all your support and compliments.

"I hated you being gone, you know," John said with a frown, "but I guess in this case it was the best thing. Now that you're back, I can see that. You're sharp as a tack and as aggressive as ever."

"You're a good man, John Billingsly, and I'm so lucky to have you for a boss."

He brightened, then said in a low tone. "I...we could be more, you know. Only you're not interested, are you?"

She gave him a sad smile. "No, not in the way you mean. But I take your interest in me as the highest of compliments."

John sighed, then smiled. "It's okay. I was prepared for a no."

"I have always considered you a friend and the best boss ever."

He hesitated for a long moment, giving her such a long look that she felt like squirming in her seat.

"What?" she asked, leaning her head to one side and returning his gaze.

"You're not the same."

Kelly's chest tightened, and she staved off a sigh. "You just got through telling me—"

"I'm not talking about your work," John interrupted.

"Oh," she said, turning away, fearing he was about to enter a forbidden zone. His next words proved her right.

"When you don't think anyone's watching, you have the saddest look on your face." He paused and angled his head. "Why is that?"

"I'm fine," she lied. "Your imagination's just working overtime."

"Baloney."

"John—"

He cut her off again. "I know I'm prying, but hell, that's what friends—and bosses—do."

"It's something I have to work through."

"Is it still your family?"

She smiled. "No, not in the way you mean. Getting away actually accomplished a remarkable thing. When I think of them, which is every day, it's with the fondest and sweetest of memories instead of pain associated with loss and heartache."

"I'm so glad to hear you say that, Kelly. That's truly wonderful."

She blinked back tears. "I know."

"But," John pressed, "you're still far too sad to suit me." He paused again and leaned forward. "It's that guy, isn't it?"

Kelly stiffened. "I don't know what guy you're talking about."

"Damn straight you do."

Trying to ward off a flush that was sure to appear in her cheeks, Kelly got up, turned her back and walked to the window. The day was gloomy and cloudy just like her spirits. John was right. She was in a funk, though she couldn't afford to admit that. Even to herself.

But heavens, she missed Grant. Not only did she miss him, she ached for him. All of him. Right now, she could envision his big rugged body in the woods wearing his hard hat, jeans and boots, operating a piece of equipment or tromping among the trees, totally immersed in what he was doing. Loving every minute of it, too.

If only he loved her with the same passion he loved the woods.

"Kelly?"

She whipped around. "Sorry. My mind was just wandering."

John frowned, then stood. "If you're not going to confide in me, then I'd best get out of here." He peered at his watch. "I'm due in court in thirty minutes, and if I'm not mistaken, so are you."

"You're right." Kelly squared her shoulders, cleared her mind of everything personal and added with grit, "This is one case I don't intend to lose."

"You won't. And, as promised, that will put you in the partner arena." When he apparently didn't get the response he wanted, his frown returned. "That's what you still want, isn't it?"

"Absolutely," Kelly said with forced enthusiasm, grabbing her briefcase, "Let's go make waves."

She'd been home only a month but it seemed like six. Her eyes swept around the living room of her condo in Houston, thinking how lucky she was to have such a lovely place to come home to every day. It just didn't seem as beautiful as it had before she'd left for Lane.

Besides this luxury, she had lots of friends and exciting places to go. Houston offered so much. It was the best.

Then why wasn't she out enjoying herself with friends? It was only six o'clock. She still had plenty of time to re- consider an invitation to a dinner theater she'd turned down earlier.

However, she didn't feel like going out. After the day she'd had in court, she wanted to soak in her tub and spend the rest of the evening reading and relaxing.

Unfortunately, that wasn't happening.

Shortly after she'd turned the key in the lock, she'd found herself uptight, anxious and lonely, all of which made her furious at herself. To make matters worse, she'd received two phone calls back to back—one from Maud and one from Ruth.

They had both told her how much they missed her, and

for her to hurry back to Lane and see them. Following both conversations, Kelly had hung up the phone, broken down and cried.

Now, as she sat with her feet curled under her on the sofa, she felt like crying some more. "Stop it," she spat out loud.

She had nothing to cry about, for God's sake. She had everything in the world going for her. In addition to this lovely home, a great job and salary, she had been offered a junior partnership in the firm, as John had predicted.

Even though she hadn't officially accepted the offer, everyone knew that she would.

Everyone except herself.

The reason being she was miserable. And it was all because of Grant. Without having all the wonderful things she had in life were just that—*things*. Since she had met Grant and fallen in love with him, things no longer seemed to matter. Sure, she still wanted to practice law, but the passion for doing that and that alone was gone. Yes, she still loved her condo, but it was just somewhere to sleep. The passion for that was gone, as well.

Her passion was Grant.

Suddenly a light clicked on inside Kelly's head. She'd rather wake up every morning with Grant beside her than anything else in the world.

She lunged to her feet and backed up to the fireplace. It was impossible! Living in a small town wasn't something she could do.

Liar, her conscience whispered. She had lived there for several weeks and survived. She had even made friends, done good work and thrived in Lane. So what did that mean?

Kelly's mind reeled as she took deep, heaving breaths,

trying to settle her rapidly beating heart and fractured nerves. Then it hit her like a knock on the head. She had lost Eddie through a tragedy she couldn't control. Not so with Grant. If she lost him, it would be her fault.

Grabbing her purse, she ran out the door.

"What's with you, anyway?" Pete asked, casting Grant a hard look.

He scowled. "Nothing."

"The hell you say. You've been acting like someone poked a hot iron up your ass."

"If you weren't my friend and I didn't need you on this job, I'd *deck* your ass."

Both men glared at each other for seconds; then they both laughed.

"Sorry, boss," Pete said. "I should've kept my mouth shut."

"Yeah, you should have. But you're right, I've got lots on my mind."

"Would that 'lots' have the initials K.B.?"

Grant hesitated, not sure how much he wanted his friend to know about his personal life. But since he'd been such a pain, Grant felt he owed Pete the truth. Or part of it, anyway.

"I miss her," Grant admitted with a sigh.

"Me, too."

"Let's get back to work."

Pete nodded.

That conversation had taken place early that morning. But although Grant worked like a Trojan soldier every day to exhaust himself, nothing could prepare him for the nights, no matter how worn-out he was.

He ached for Kelly. At every turn, he smelled her, heard her laughter, felt her skin under his callused fingers. But the worst was remembering the moans she made when he made love to her. That, and all the other special things about her, drove him mad.

He loved her, dammit. He should've told her that. He bounded off the couch, went to the kitchen, and grabbed a beer. After one swig, he poured it down the sink. Getting drunk wasn't the answer. When he came out of his stupor, Kelly would still be haunting him.

It was too late, anyhow. Or was it?

He made his way back into the living room, stood there a second, then muttered, "To hell with this."

He dashed to his desk and grabbed an envelope, reached for his jacket, then walked out of the cabin.

Kelly saw him the instant she stepped outside. While her heart dropped to her toes, she pulled up short and watched like a zombie as Grant walked across the condo parking lot, stopping just short of touching her.

"What…what are you doing here?"

"Where are you going?" Grant answered with a question.

"I asked first." Her voice came out a whisper.

"I came to see you." His eyes delved into hers.

"Why?"

He rocked back on his heels and took a deep breath. "To tell you that I love you and that I'm one miserable bastard without you."

Suddenly her excitement reached a feverish pitch. "I was on my way to see you, to tell you the same thing."

Later, Kelly had no idea who moved first. It didn't

matter. Within seconds, they were locked in each other's arms. Then, laughing and kissing her, he lifted her and swung her around.

Once he put her down, he kissed her gently on the lips, then whispered, "Marry me, Kelly Baker."

At three o'clock the following morning, Kelly and Grant sat cross-legged in the middle of Kelly's king-size bed, drinking ginger ale and munching on cheese and crackers.

They had made love until both were exhausted and starving. Naked, they had made their way into the kitchen where they grabbed whatever was handy in the refrigerator, then carried it back to bed.

Now, as they stared deep into each other's eyes and drank their ginger ale, Kelly felt Grant's free hand grasp hers and squeeze. She returned the squeeze, then reached for his glass and set both of them on the bedside table.

"I love you, Grant Wilcox."

"And I love you, Kelly Baker."

"So when is the wedding?" She blinked back unplanned tears.

He traced her lips with a finger. "How 'bout tomorrow?"

Extra blood rushed into her cheeks. "I wish."

"Me, too. But just as soon as we get the legal red tape out of the way, there'll be no stopping us."

"I hope not."

Grant cleared his throat. "I never thought I could live in civilization again, but with you as my wife, I know it's possible."

With tears flowing, Kelly leaned over, kissed him then

repeated a version of his words. "I never thought I could live in the woods and practice law, but with you as my husband, it's possible. In fact, that's what I want to do."

"You love me that much that you'd consider giving all this up?" Grant's voice held awe.

"In a heartbeat."

Grant moaned deeply, and reached for her again and held her so tightly she couldn't breathe. But that was all right with her.

Finally, he pulled back and said, "I love you so much I want to crawl inside you."

"And I you."

"I have something for you." Releasing her, he leaned over and reached for his jeans.

She watched as he removed something from one of the pockets. "What it that?"

"Open it and see."

She did, then gazed at him with a puzzled expression on her face. "It's a deed, I know. But to what?"

"The house in Wellington."

She gave him an incredulous look.

"I'd heard it was up for sale, and sure enough it was," he added.

"So you bought it." Her voice was barely audible.

"Yep. For you. For us."

Kelly let out a cry and threw her arms around his neck, landing kisses all over his face.

He laughed. "I take it I did good buying it?"

"You did better than good. You did perfect."

"After you said you liked it, I called a Realtor friend and had him check out the rumors about it being on the market." Grant held up his hand. "Don't get me wrong, I had no idea you loved me, but something told me to buy that house, no matter what."

"Oh, Grant, it's wonderful And Wellington will be perfect for us—it's big enough for me to set up a practice."

"Without a doubt."

"I've always wanted to own my own firm someday."

"That day is here. Today."

"And it's a perfect place to raise a family." She waited with bated breath for his response.

His eyes suddenly misted with tears. Her heart turned over.

"I was afraid you wouldn't want another child." His voice was strained.

"Oh, but I do," she said with a tremor. "As a matter of—"

He placed his hands on her shoulders, stopping her flow of words, and gently eased her back onto the bed. "Then we'd best get started, my love, 'cause time's a-wasting."

Kelly grinned, looped her arms around his neck, drew him down to her and whispered, "I think the first one's already a done deal."

He pulled back with awe written on his face. "You…you mean—" He gulped.

She smiled with her heart and gave him a deep kiss. When she eased back, she whispered, "That's exactly what I mean."

With tears in his eyes, Grant hugged her fiercely and cried, "I love you, I love you, I love you."

"I love you, too."

* * * * *

What Happens in Vegas...

Their Million-Dollar Night

by

KATHERINE GARBERA

(SD #1720)

Roxy O'Malley is just the kind of hostess corporate sophisticate Max Williams needs for some R & R while at the casinos. Will one white-hot night lead to a trip to the altar?

Don't miss the exciting conclusion to WHAT HAPPENS IN VEGAS... available this April from Silhouette Desire.

On Sale April 2006
Available at your favorite retail outlet.

**He's proud, passionate, primal—dare
she surrender to the sheikh?**

Feel warm winds blowing through your hair
and the hot desert sun on your skin as you are transported
to exotic lands…. As the temperature rises, let yourself be
seduced by our sexy, irresistible sheikhs.

In *Traded to the Sheikh* by Emma Darcy,
Emily Ross is the prisoner of Sheikh Zageo bin
Sultan al Farrahn—he seems to think she'll
trade her body for her freedom! Emily must
prove her innocence before time runs out….

TRADED TO THE SHEIKH

on sale April 2006.

If you enjoyed what you just read,
then we've got an offer you can't resist!

Take 2 bestselling
love stories FREE!
Plus get a FREE surprise gift!

Clip this page and mail it to Silhouette Reader Service™

IN U.S.A.	IN CANADA
3010 Walden Ave.	P.O. Box 609
P.O. Box 1867	Fort Erie, Ontario
Buffalo, N.Y. 14240-1867	L2A 5X3

YES! Please send me 2 free Silhouette Desire® novels and my free surprise gift. After receiving them, if I don't wish to receive anymore, I can return the shipping statement marked cancel. If I don't cancel, I will receive 6 brand-new novels every month, before they're available in stores! In the U.S.A., bill me at the bargain price of $3.80 plus 25¢ shipping and handling per book and applicable sales tax, if any*. In Canada, bill me at the bargain price of $4.47 plus 25¢ shipping and handling per book and applicable taxes**. That's the complete price and a savings of at least 10% off the cover prices—what a great deal! I understand that accepting the 2 free books and gift places me under no obligation ever to buy any books. I can always return a shipment and cancel at any time. Even if I never buy another book from Silhouette, the 2 free books and gift are mine to keep forever.

225 SDN DZ9F
326 SDN DZ9G

Name	(PLEASE PRINT)	
Address	Apt.#	
City	State/Prov.	Zip/Postal Code

Not valid to current Silhouette Desire® subscribers.

Want to try two free books from another series?
Call 1-800-873-8635 or visit www.morefreebooks.com.

* Terms and prices subject to change without notice. Sales tax applicable in N.Y.
** Canadian residents will be charged applicable provincial taxes and GST.
   All orders subject to approval. Offer limited to one per household.
   ® are registered trademarks owned and used by the trademark owner and or its licensee.

DES04R   ©2004 Harlequin Enterprises Limited

**It's a
SUMMER OF SECRETS**

Expecting Lonergan's Baby

(#1719)

by

MAUREEN CHILD

He'd returned only for the summer…until a
passionate encounter with a sensual stranger
has this Lonergan bachelor contemplating
forever…and fatherhood.

**Don't miss the SUMMER OF SECRETS trilogy,
beginning in April from Silhouette Desire.**

On sale April 2006
Available at your favorite retail outlet!

COMING NEXT MONTH

#1717 THE FORBIDDEN TWIN—Susan Crosby
The Elliotts
Seducing your twin sister's ex-fiancé by pretending to be her…
not the best idea. Unless he succumbs.

#1718 THE TEXAN'S FORBIDDEN AFFAIR—
Peggy Moreland
A Piece of Texas
He swept her off her feet, then destroyed her. Now he wants her
back!

#1719 EXPECTING LONERGAN'S BABY—
Maureen Child
Summer of Secrets
He was home just for the summer—until a night of explosive
passion gave him a reason to stay.

#1720 THEIR MILLION-DOLLAR NIGHT—
Katherine Garbera
What Happens in Vegas…
This businessman has millions at stake in a deal but one woman
has him risking scandal and damning the consequences!

#1721 BABY, I'M YOURS—Catherine Mann
It was only supposed to be a weekend affair, then an unexpected
pregnancy changed all of the rules.

#1722 THE SOLDIER'S SEDUCTION—
Anne Marie Winston
She thought the man who'd taken her innocence was gone
forever…until he returned home to claim her—and the daughter
he never knew existed.

SDCNM0306